THE PRIESTESSES
OF MYLITTA

JANE DE LA VAUDÈRE (1857-1908) was baptized Jeanne Scrive and was married to Camille Gaston Crapez, who began styling himself Crapez de La Vaudère after inheriting the Château de La Vaudère from his mother. Her prolific literary work is very various but she was assimilated to the Decadent Movement firstly because of two scandalously scabrous Parisian novels, *Les Demi-Sexes* (1897) and *Les Androgynes*(1903), and, more pertinently, because of a series of accounts of moeurs antiques, some of which—notably *Le Mystère de Kama* (1901)—set new standards of excess.

BRIAN STABLEFORD's scholarly work includes *New Atlantis: A Narrative History of Scientific Romance* (Wildside Press, 2016), *The Plurality of Imaginary Worlds: The Evolution of French roman scientifique* (Black Coat Press, 2017) and *Tales of Enchantment and Disenchantment: A History of Faerie* (Black Coat Press, 2019). He has translated more than three hundred volumes from the French, mostly in the genres of *roman scientifique*, *contes de fées* and Romantic and Symbolist fiction. His recent fiction includes the visionary science fiction novel *The Revelations of Time and Space* (2020) and its sequel *After the Revelation* (2021); the last in his long series of "Tales of the Genetic Revolution," *The Elusive Shadows* (2020); and the comedy fantasy *Meat on the Bone* (2021), all published by Snuggly Books.

I0591609

JANE DE LA VAUDÈRE

THE PRIESTESSES OF MYLITTA

TRANSLATED AND WITH AN INTRODUCTION BY
BRIAN STABLEFORD

THIS IS A SNUGGLY BOOK

ISBN: 978-1-64525-089-0

CONTENTS

INTRODUCTION

THE present volume is an addendum to a set of six volumes featuring the work of Jane de La Vaudère (1857-1908); regrettably, no copy was available to me when I translated those volumes, but I was able to purchase one subsequently. *Les Prêtresses de Mylitta* (1907) was the last novel published during the author's lifetime, although it was followed by a novelette published in volume form, *Rêve de Myses* (1908; tr. as "The Dream of Myses"), also published by Albert Méricant and similarly illustrated with photographs of naked women, which the publisher was trying hard to promote as a new art form. The book is now scarce because of that unusual fashion of illustration (all the plates had been excised from the copy that I was able to buy for translation).

Les Prêtresses de Mylitta makes use of groundwork laid in the author's previous novel, *La Vierge d'Israel* (1906; tr. as "The Virgin of Israel"), similarly set in Babylon in a slightly later period of its history, to which it forms a "prequel" of sorts. *La Vierge d'Israel* is set immediately before the fall of Babylon, and its climax

7

describes the episode in the Biblical Book of *Daniel* that features Belshazzar's feast and the supernatural writing on the wall that interrupts it. *Les Prêtresses de Mylitta* touches on an earlier Biblical prophecy first featured in *Jeremiah* and repeated in *Daniel*, regarding the fate of Nebuchnadnezzar, whose army conquered Judah, captured Jerusalem and looted the Temple, thus allegedly incurring the wrath of Jehovah. Although the novel makes reference to the prophecy in question, however, it makes no substantial employment of it in the plot, which is entirely fictitious and focuses narrowly, as the title implies, on the temple of Mylitta and an event unrecorded by history.

"Mylitta" is a name attributed to a Babylonian goddess by the unreliable historian Herodotus, a great believer in traveler's tales, to whom we owe the allegation that Babylonian law required the wives of the city to prostitute themselves there once during their life, in circumstances faithfully copied by La Vaudère in the novel. Herodotus also claims that Mylitta was the Babylonian name of the Greek goddess Aphrodite—which La Vaudère, following normal French practice at the time, gives in Romanized form as Venus. Modern archeology has found no trace of Mylitta, but some commentators suggest that the name might be derived from that of the goddess Mullissu, wife of the god Ashur. Modern accounts allege that the Babylonian goddess who had the responsibilities credited in the novel to Mylitta, at the time when the story is set, was Ishtar, whose name had replaced that of the Sumerian goddess Inanna, and who is generally considered to be the model of the

Phoenician goddess Astarte. The famous story of Ishtar's descent into the underworld is mentioned briefly by La Vaudére, and credited to Mylitta.

Mythological accuracy is, however, of scant importance in the novel, as the image of the temple of Mylitta and its rites, save for the elements taken from Herodotus, are entirely derived from La Vaudére's eternal obsession with young dancing girls enacting symbolic representations of sexual intercourse alongside more brutal sexual exploitation. Indeed, the entire novel is repetitive of her constant preoccupations with sex and torture, repeating gruesome scenes previously located in Babylon in *La Vierge d'Israel* and echoing bloody depictions in earlier novels set in India and Siam. The plot is more complex than that of its immediate predecessor, however, by virtue of the introduction of the character of Menonia, who has no equivalent in *La Vierge d'Israel*, and whose role also adds an extra melodramatic twist to the part played in *L'Amazone du roi de Siam* (1902; tr. as *The King of Siam's Amazon*) by Xali, with which it has some similarities.

It seems not unlikely that *Les Prêtresses de Mylitta* was commissioned by Méricant in the cause of his crusade to promote nude photography as an art form, and it was heavily advertised in the two periodicals featuring nude photographs that he was publishing at the time, copies of which can now be seen on *gallica*, although the various novels that reproduced the photographs as illustrations cannot. Although the association of the photographs with the story was probably entirely gratuitous—that is certainly the case with *Rêve de Myses*—Méricant must have specified that the story ought to feature a great deal of nudity, and might well have requested the inclusion of one or two of the key scenes involving Ahmosis and Menonia. (*Rêve de Myses* also features a character called Ahmosis, but she is very different from the Ahmosis of *Les Prêtresses de Mylitta*, not lending herself nearly as well to pictorial representation.)

Whether it was written to commission or not, however, the novel works as well, as a narrative stripped of its illustrations, as any of La Vaudère's novels, and perhaps better than some, in that its conclusion, although typically clipped and hasty, gives the impression of having been planned in advance rather more carefully than some of its predecessors, with careful groundwork for its narrative twists laid well before. If it seemed less shocking than its predecessors when it was first published, that is because shock value tends to wear off rapidly; to any reader who had not previously read *Le Mystère de Kama* (1901; tr. as "The Mystery of Kama"), *L'Amazone du roi de Siam* and *La Vierge d'Israel* it would have seemed very shocking indeed, and the same is true today. Anyone who has read the six-volume set of the author's translated works might well consider this addendum to be simply more of the same, while anyone who has not read anything else by the author will probably find it mind-boggling that such a novel could be written and published in 1907 by a small, seemingly frail woman in her fifties who died soon afterwards, in circumstances carefully unspecified by the newspapers that reported her death.

La Vaudère went on to enjoy a moderately substantial posthumous career, but the novels with her signature published after her death were probably written some time before; if appearances can be trusted, she might well have packaged up several unsold novels and sent them to Méricant before dying, leaving it to him to dispose of them as he wished. *Rêve de Myses* gives the impression of having been written some years before—prior to or in parallel with *L'Amant du Pharaon* (1905; tr. as "Pharaoh's Lover"), which includes some identical passages—and so do two other works included with *Rêve de Myses* in the list of the author's works featured in the prefatory material of *Les Prêtresses de Mylitta* after *La Vierge d'Israel, La Porte de Félicité* and *L'Invincible Amour*; although the editions are undated, their publication probably did not precede *Les Prêtresses de Mylitta*. A poetic version of *Rêve de Myses* advertised on the same page never appeared.

Les *Prêtresses de Mylitta* was, therefore, at least very probably, the author's last completed work, the concluding flourish, if not a kind of summation, of the aspect of her career dealing with *moeurs antiques* [ancient mores]; although it repeats all her central obsessions, it also represents them more starkly, and perhaps a little more frankly, than she had thought it diplomatic to do previously. Although it might well have been an item of commercial work, written in a fashion deliberately calculated to please the readers who had awarded her with bestseller status since the publication of *Le Mystère de Kama*, there is nothing half-hearted about it, and no sign that she was not as intensely emotionally involved with the project as she generally seemed to be—with the possible exception of the slightly surprising ending, which is not typical of her normal procedure, although it certainly fits the story esthetically. As to what the story might tell us about the author's own attitude to sex and death, or exactly what effect she might have been hoping to have on her readers' attitudes to those serious matters, we can, of course, only speculate.

The translation was made from a copy of the Méricant edition, which is undated, but was definitely published in 1907, as it was reviewed then in several newspapers as well as being advertised as available in Méricant's contemporary periodicals.

—Brian Stableford

THE PRIESTESSES
OF MYLITTA

PART ONE

I

IN the temple consecrated to her, she was seen standing on a bull, wearing a starry tiara and streaming with jewels. Her hair descended over her shoulders in curly ringlets; she was holding a bow and quiver.

When she represented the goddess of generation, the reproduction of mortal beings, she was naked and smiling, placing her hands over her breasts in a modest gesture.

The women of Babylon came to adore "the Lady of Life" who watched over them. They went to the temple in order to deliver themselves at least once, after their marriage, to a haphazard lover. The richest were drawn in sumptuous carriages and, breasts bare and their heads circled by a cord, they summoned the elect of the goddess, shuddering with sensual pleasure.

That day, the temple was full of men and women who were waiting in a meditative attitude for the habitual ceremony of sales and exchanges, for the nubile girls offered on the terraces of the temple by expert matrons who detailed their charms.

A public crier put the beauty of the virgins up for auction, commencing with the most accomplished. From that one, sold at an advantageous price, he passed on to the next, still very well made and desirable, and those sales of human flesh became veritable unions, which were concluded to the liking of everyone.

The fortunate espousers bid enthusiastically, detailing the perfections of the feminine livestock submitted to their appreciation, praising the delicacy of the joints, the flexibility of the limbs, the ease of the gait and the expression of the face.

The beautiful creatures of amour rapidly found a buyer and drew away in a halo of glory to take possession of their new dwelling. As for the ugly, the disgraced and the deformed, their fate was less enviable, for the thrifty males who bought them cheap counted primarily on making them labor in the fields and in the household. But almost all the virgins presented in the temple of Mylitta found a buyer sooner or later.

While the crowd flowed slowly toward the auction that was about to begin, a girl lying in front of the image of the goddess was weeping abundantly. With crafty movements, an old woman was striving to remove the garments from the child, who was already almost naked, save for a coral hood whose roseate stones were trembling over her cheeks.

"I don't want to! I don't want to!" she sighed, amid her sobs. "I'm not old enough to be sold."

The old woman laughed disdainfully. "Younger ones than you have been auctioned. With your muzzle of an amorous cat you'll be able to charm a rich man, who'll pay a good price for you. I'm poor, and at my age, it's hard to labor."

"It's Starzo that I love."

"Starzo won't be able to buy you at the prince you're worth. He doesn't own anything except his skiff and his oarsman's arms. Even if he offered his frail boat and the produce of several miraculous catches, he wouldn't be able to accumulate the sum I require."

The girl wrung her slender hands and beat her breast.

"I don't want to be sold! You know full well, Morphy, that one can't dispose of a girl before her fifteenth year, and I won't reach that age for another two months."

Priestesses were passing through the temple carrying flowers and perfumes. They were perfectly beautiful young women with parted hair woven into supple braids that fell over each shoulder. Golden plaques put yellow gleams over their brown cheeks and long crimson veils hung down to their heels in harmonious pleats. They sang and danced for the goddess, equally happy to distract mortals after having sacrificed to the cult of Mylitta.

"Why are you weeping?" one of them asked the desolate child.

"I'm weeping," the child said, "because Morphy wants to sell me at auction, and I'm not old enough."

"Is Morphy your mother?"

"No," said the old woman, "but I've given my cares to Ahmosis, who no longer has any parents. I picked her up when she was two years old, and no one has ever reclaimed her, so she's mine. Should I not compensate myself today for the trouble she's given me?"

"Indeed," said the priestess, "but can't you wait a little longer?"

"No, for I have no more provisions in the house. Already, we had to go without a meal this morning."

Ahmosis embraced the young woman's knees. "Keep me in the temple," she moaned. "I'll be your servant."

She was exquisite thus, with her short hair mingled with the rosy beads of the coral hood. Her large dark eyes, with tapering arched eyebrows and mauve-tinted eyelids lent a passionate expression to the dainty, almost puerile face. The small mouth, lips slightly parted, swelled for further sobs; the thin nostrils quivered.

"I'd like to keep you with me," said the priestess, gently, "but unfortunately, I couldn't pay the price for you this woman is asking. Even my jewels belong to Mylitta. However, if destiny treats you cruelly subsequently, you only have to come to the temple, where you'll find me."

"Truly?" said Ahmosis. "You won't forget me? What's your name?"

"My name is Menonia; I'm a musician and dancer."

The young woman had already rejoined her companions, and Morphy obliged the child to get up, rudely.

II

THE temple stood on the bank of the river, from which it was only separated by its terraces. A curious, noisy crowd was swarming around it, awaiting the hour of the sale of the virgins. The women's torsos were swathed in yellow- or green-striped cloth, showing their arms and legs the color of baked clay, ornamented by broad rings of ivory and glass. The men had beards with spiral curls, and their heads were decked with white tiaras maintained by a metal circle. Brightly-colored fringed robes descended over their calves.

Morphy dragged Ahmosis on to the terraces, but the best places were already occupied and it was necessary to be content with a stall at the back, devoid of a platform and drapery.

The pretty girls were exhibited in the front rows, amorous livestock lying among flowers on precious fabrics, their hair mingled with roses, their eyes enlarged and their lips painted. All of them hoped to find a rich buyer, likeable and grandiose, so they had made the most of their natural graces, substituting for slight imperfections by means of savant poses and engaging smiles. The small raised themselves up on piles of cushions; the thin leaned forward slightly in order to make their small breasts stand out; opulent beauties stretched themselves limply, their hands joined behind the neck, the entire body an amorous offering.

Morphy handled Ahmosis roughly, who resisted with all her strength, refusing to lie down amid the fabrics and cushions with the virginal livestock displayed before the attentive eyes of the male connoisseurs.

"Stay there," she said, pushing the child into a narrow box furnished with a thin hemp mattress. "Stand up when the men approach you, and answer their questions meekly."

In the neighboring boxes, the girls laughed at Ahmosis' resistance.

"Are you scared of being eaten, then?"

"A woman who knows what she's doing easily gets a husband."

"You'll certainly be happier than with Morphy, who beats you incessantly."

"I'm not old enough to be sold," the girl repeated, "and I want to choose a man myself."

"All men are alike. It's only necessary to ask them for the pleasure of a kiss and the satisfaction of money. Before the embrace, demand a new jewel, for sated desire is often forgetful. Let each of your caresses cost an advantageous price, and never accord anything by virtue of the generosity of the soul, no matter how tempted you are!"

The beautiful girls quivered on their silky fabrics; they felt vibrant, overexcited like mares in the evening of a stormy day. A spicy tremor ran over their supple limbs; they showed their gleaming teeth in nervous laughter.

"Personally," said Hermeriah, a virgin with russet eyes whose skin had golden and coppery reflections, "I want to be loved every evening, and I'll have slaves to serve me. I'll never spoil my little hands with vile housework."

"We're beautiful enough," sighed Timmouz, displaying her glorious body on crimson and silvery drapery, "to live without doing anything."

"When we've given sensual pleasure to men, we have a right to their gratitude," said Hermeriah, whose eyes were ablaze. "The one who chooses me will know all the savor of intercourse; but he'll be coaxing and submissive."

A young woman who was kneeling, one leg folded under the thigh and the other forming an acute angle, by virtue of being accustomed to playing short Assyrian harps, put her hands together ecstatically.

"For myself, I shall adore the man who deigns to take me. My husband will have no meeker and more obedient slave than his little Ranis."

"And he'll despise you," said Timmouz, disdainfully. "Doubtless you'll also play him languorous tunes and sing your tenderness to all the echoes in the house?"

A girl whose heavy hair made her seem very slight, was nibbling sweetmeats from the palm of her hand. "Personally," she said, "I want my husband to give me delicate dishes every day, snowy sorbets and flowery preserves. Afterwards, I'll cherish him."

23

But the public crier was commencing the sale.

Men of every species and every condition were gathered there. They circulated between the florid boxes examining the items, palpating them, stroking them, looking at their eyes and their teeth like experts. As they approached, the girls surrounding Ahmosis fell silent, glad if the gaze of the connoisseurs was directed toward them.

III

THIS is what Herodotus says about the laws of Babylon, in this regard:

In every district, those who had nubile daughters brought them to a place where a great many men gathered around them. A public crier made them stand up and sold them all, one after another. He began with the most beautiful and, after having obtained a considerable sum, he proclaimed these who were nearest to her, but he only sold them on the condition that the buyers married them.

All the rich Babylonians who were of age bid against one another in order to buy the most beautiful. As for the youths of the people, as they had less need to marry beautiful women than to have a wife who would bring them a dowry, they took the ugliest, with the money that was given with them.

In fact, the crier had no sooner finished selling the beautiful than he made the ugliest stand up, or one who was crippled, advertising her at the lowest price, asking who wanted to marry her on that condition and awarding her to anyone who made the promise. The money given came from the beauties, and a part of that sum endowed the ugly and the crippled.

It was not permitted to parents to choose a husband for their daughter, and a man who had bought a girl could not take her home until he had given a guarantee of marrying her. When he had found guarantors he took her to his house. In cases where two spouses were in disagreement, the law sided with the one who had paid the money. It was also permitted for people from another town, without distinction, to come to the sale and to buy one of the young women if he wished.

On a platform higher than the others, the crier invited the virgins to emerge from their boxes, calling them by their names.

"Hermeriah!" he said, letting his ivory hammer fall.

The girl with the russet eyes and the polished coppery skin stood up slowly, sticking out her firm, round and pointed breasts.

An approving murmur ran through the crowd. That slender and sinewy body pleased the hedonists fatigued by countless orgies. The spicy beauty of the virgin re-awakened extinct desires.

"Sixty minims!" said the crier.

"Two talents!"

"Three talents!"

"Ten talents!"

The bids rose up and the young woman, arching her back, swiveled slowly, smiling, in order to show herself from all angles.

She was sold for twenty talents to a rich merchant, who took her away immediately, after having thrown a thick veil over her shoulders in order to hide her from the gazes of the people.

"Timmouz!" said the crier, letting his hammer fall in order to demand silence.

The virgin quit her crimson and silver bed nonchalantly. She had harmoniously rounded hips, a neat and firm rump and breasts erect in amorous battle order. Her plump and gleaming arms were already extended like rubber bands for the embrace.

"Two talents!"

"Five talents!"

As for Hermeriah, the connoisseurs were numerous. Timmouz, in the flower of youth, was bound to please all men, for her beauty was perfect. She swayed like an amber serpent, her slender torso inclined, her lips twisting toward imminent kisses.

"Hatasoun!" said the crier.

That one had blazing dark eyes and red lips that laughed incessantly. She was sold for ten gold talents to an officer in the royal militia.

Then came the submissive Ranis, whose modest air designed her to the choice of a teacher of cuneiform writing.

At each sale the witnesses placed the mark of their seal or the impression of their fingernail in the wax next to those of the buyer and the seller. Mercantile passion was innate in the Babylonians, but they brought a great patience and rectitude to its satisfaction.

The virgins filed before the platform of the crier Amounnzou. A few, although disgraced by nature, had beautiful nostalgic eyes widely separated by the nose of an idol with narrow nostrils. Others, scarcely formed, still boyish and turbulent, leapt like kittens, showing their pointed teeth. Girls of a bestial type, with squat heads and prominent cheekbones advanced awkwardly and followed men of the people who paid a minimal price.

All the amorous livestock had been placed and the crier was about to retire when Morphy abruptly surged forth on to the platform.

"There's still one girl to sell," she said.

Surprised Amounnzou considered the old woman. "Her name isn't on my tablets."

"That's because I only decided at the last minute. I was just about to make the declaration to you when the sale began. Get up, Ahmosis."

Ahmosis, her eyes shiny with tears, stood up slowly.

"She's beautiful," said the crier, "but I don't know who to offer her to; all the connoisseurs have gone."

"Try anyway," said the old woman, humbly. "Perhaps a buyer will present himself."

A young man came forward eagerly. "Me," he said.

The newcomer did not have the wavy and curly beard of the Assyrians; his cheeks were smooth, and the perfect oval of his face differed essentially from the prominent cheekbones, the thick lips and the broad mask that Babylonians normally presented. His violet-blue eyes scintillated between dark eyelids. His fine silky hair was parted in soft waves, and all the particularities of his person composed a proud beauty that Ahmosis had not resisted.

"Who are you?" asked the crier.

"I'm Starzo, the boatman."

"He doesn't have anything," said Morphy, disdainfully. "His skiff is the most wretched on the river, and see how he's dressed!"

"One gold minim," said Amounnzou. "That isn't too dear?"

"I don't have it, alas."

"What are you offering, then?"

"My skiff and its oars, its crimson cushions and its awning. I also have good fishing-nets."

"His boat takes in water everywhere and his oars are white wood. As for its cushions and its awning, the sun laughs through all the rips. Rags that a dog wouldn't want!" cried Morphy.

Strarzo clenched his fists under the insult. "I have my youth," he said, "and my ardor for labor."

"A sad contribution, while time is short."

"I would adore Ahmosis like the goddess of grace and pleasure. No wife would be as happy ..."

"A wife is only happy by virtue of situation and fortune," said Morphy. "With what would you offer yours jewels, perfumes, gold and silver veils—all the trifles, in sum, that render us glorious?"

"I'll be able to satisfy the desires of Ahmosis."

"You'll be a murderer and a thief, then!"

"Shut up!" cried Starzo, throwing himself upon the old woman. "Ahmosis isn't your daughter; you have no rights over her. Let her designate the husband of her choice, then. I swear to submit myself to her will."

Ahmosis turned her beautiful eyes toward the young man. "I want to be Starzo's," she said. "I give myself to him."

At that moment, there was a great stir among the people, who flooded toward the terraces. Bands of men, women and children passed by, shouting, preceding a troop of militia, a guard of honor whose golden bonnets and long red plumes were visible. The indigenous host was mingled with various specimens of exotic races: hairy Ethiopians, torsos garnished with leather thongs; Pelasgians clad in tiger- or leopard-skins; Asiatics with the tint of ripe lemons and long beards curled and twisted into slender cords; negroes from the upper Nile covered in ivory and copper ornaments. Soldiers with bucklers on their backs and bronze axes in their hands surrounded an individual coiffed in an imposing tiara and draped with a fringed robe decorated with embroideries.

"May Lord Ahassuru live forever!"[1] howled the joyful crowd.

Beautiful women stopped, smiling, scintillating with enamels, pearls and gold. They took flowers from their hair in order to throw them at the powerful satrap, who inclined toward them his long emblematic cane terminated by a silver eagle with its wings outspread.

Ahassuru came to the market of virgins, but he seemed disappointed when he saw the empty boxes and the crier Amounnzou inscribing the product of the sale on his wax tablet.

---

1 Ahassuru is an alternative spelling of the name Ahasuerus, given to a king in the Biblical book of *Esther*, identified by most commentators as Xerxes I, who ruled the Persian Empire from 486 B.C. until his assassination in 465 B.C. The fictitious character given that name here, however, is of more modest status, living in an earlier era.

"I've arrived too late," he said, with annoyance. "Is there no girl left to cede?"

Amounnzou prostrated himself before the satrap and kissed the hem of his mantle. "May your lordship be glorious forever!"

However, Ahassuru had perceived Ahmosis, whom the old woman was maintaining at the foot of the platform with an iron hand. "Is that child for sale?" he demanded, interestedly.

"Certainly, my dear master," said Morphy, swiftly. "This child is the most accomplished of the virgins of Babylon. See how she is made! Her flesh is honeyed, her body flawless. She sings and can play the nine-stringed harp like the priestesses of Mylitta. Make the acquisition of her for some chief of your militia. You'll be satisfied!"

Amounnzou, rendered very eager by the hope of profit, supported what the old woman said. "I've kept her for you," he said, brazenly, "for she was my purest jewel. I thought that she would excite your desire. The others, you see, were unworthy of your favor."

Ahmosis, her eyes widened by dread and horror, remained motionless. Her svelte body was displayed in its juvenile suavity. One of her hands partly veiled her round pure breasts, the other hid more mysterious beauties.

The satrap admired the slenderness of the tapering fingers, the elegance of the narrow feet, the slimness of the waist, the charming roundness of the thighs and the proud grace of the voluptuously elongated leg. That form, of a gracility that was still child-like, charmed the man, jaded by rare but imperious desires.

"I'll buy the girl," he said.

Ahmosis knelt down in an attitude of desolation and prayer. "Have pity, dear lord! I'm not old enough to be sold."

The satrap laughed heartily. "So much the better," he said. "Your kiss will be all the sweeter for it." And as Starzo advanced, his eyes shining and a menace on his lips, he struck the young man with his silver stick and added: "Someone chastise this beggar!"

Quicker than the soldiers, however, the boatman ran away into the temple, where the priestesses were dancing before the idol. The crowd had deserted the terraces in order to witness the ceremonies of the worship of Mylitta. In order to encourage the beautiful young women fluttering before the golden statue of the Lady of Sensual Pleasure, people were uttering frenetic exclamations that made the entire edifice vibrate.

The short, violently perfumed hair of the dancing girls floated over their shoulders; their bare feet struck the floor, sometimes with a weary and idle slowness, sometimes with an impatient ardor. Their hips swayed, undulating softly, while their extended arms accentuated the lascivious rhythm, rising and falling like tremulous wings.

Menonia, the star mime, was soon disengaged from the group, and, as if attracted by an invincible lover, bore her gaze toward Starzo, who was kneeling at the foot of the idol, knowing that that refuge was inviolable. Menonia, her eyes half-closed, spun gracefully around the altar, expressing an entire passionate poem that the ecstatic faithful understood.

Sometimes, the young woman tilted her head back, flexing her entire body with an incomparable suppleness and then straightening up by means of a charming movement. She seemed to be offering her gentlest gestures to the handsome boatman, whom she was seeing for the first time, and whom she was yearning to know better, unable to explain his singular audacity.

The profane, in fact, never penetrated into the center of the temple, reserved for officiants, and Zazai, the High Priestess, was only waiting for the end of the dance to expel the reckless individual. She was enveloped in her roseate veil, as a sign of wrath, and her hand, ornamented with precious rings, was raised in a gesture of fear and protestation.

Starzo had doubtless understood the mute anathema, for it was in vain that Menonia, with her most exquisite pirouette, sought him at the foot of the goddess with an engaging and tender gaze.

IV

WITH all the force of her frail arms, Ahmosis repelled her abductors, but at a sign from the satrap, two slaves carried her on to the broad quay of bricks, and, after having bound and gagged her, they deposited her in a boat with a decorative golden awning. A bright sail embroidered with chimerical birds was quivering at the upright mast. The rudder was composed of two gigantic oars terminated by the head of Oannes, the Chaldean fish-god.

Ahassuru took his place beside the girl, and when the mooring-rope was untied, the boat drew away rapidly along the river, dividing with its prow the aggregation of primitive vessels, rafts sustained by inflated skins, and skiffs painted white, red and green. A few boats were terminated at each extremity by lions, winged bulls with human faces, or fantastic and terrible emblems. Others consisted simply of long strips of bark maintained by cords, more or less, and steered by means of a paddle.

A strong breeze impelled the boat under the blazing sun, which scorched the quays and the monstrous edifices on the banks of the Euphrates. The ferocious sun filled the sky and made the river resemble a burning, soft and ruddy band of molten metal.

And a crushing, irresistible annihilation descended upon the despair of Ahmosis. Her thoughts gradually arrested, her will falling into an invincible torpor. She no longer saw the tawny man with the woven beard who was leaning over her; she no longer heard his hoarse voice and his coarse laughter.

She was naked, however, abandoned to the covetousness of a master, and nothing could preserve her from the imminent violation.

The boat was now passing under the blazing monuments more rapidly. The city of lust and crime was displayed in all its indecent magnificence. To begin with, there was the ancient part, the center of civilization, the heart of the city, where the temple of Mylitta, the Lady of Sensual Pleasure, was located. Alongside it stood the royal city, with its palaces protected by immense walls. To the north was the city of Cutha, comprising the treasure and the temple of Nirgal, to the south the city of Borsippa, with its acropolis and the great tower of Bit-Zida. A little further away the hanging gardens extended, the prodigious creation of flowers and verdure, which was not the work of Semiramis but that of a Syrian king sufficiently amorous to execute the bizarre caprice of a mad mistress.

Ahassuru did not even glance at the ruins of Babil, formidable and desolate, or the Kasr, crowned by its enormous platform. Absorbed by the contemplation of Ahmosis, he did not notice, either, that a young man had been following them, swimming, since the second water-gate.

That was Starzo, who, not having been able to get back to his boat, had let himself slide into the river. He stretched his arms over the waves with reflections of gold, following at a distance the boat that was carrying away his heart.

He had been swimming feverishly for an hour, but it was necessary to increase his efforts as the current became more rapid. His respiration was wheezing and halting, and a higher wave sometimes covered his forehead with foam. It seemed to him that the banks were spinning, and his anguish rose to a furious gallop and a vertiginous race toward the abyss. Tall rushes clung to him, rolling gusts of scent like caresses. He was breathing an odor of aromatics and corruption that made him feel faint. His veins were seething increasingly; he saw red disks passing through the blurred water of the river, and only his immense amour still sustained his will.

Perhaps the boat was about to land? The river was no longer more than a few brasses wide, and the shade of morbid vegetation gave it a little coolness. Starzo suspended himself, his hands clutching a hanging branch, and rested momentarily. The grandiose constructions were succeeded by wretched hovels of raw brick; sordid huts of dried mud and straw seemed to swell the soil with unequal blisters from which rare human ants emerged.

Ahassuru had untied the girl's bonds. Leaning over her, he inhaled the pure breath of her lips, attempting audacious caresses. He had fled the murderous radiation, the frightful flow of the cauldron of incandescent gold, and, sheltered by tall moist reeds, he sensed his desire for possession vibrating more forcefully.

Ahmosis was as luminous in her beauty as the sky, the water and the banks. Her skin seemed to have captured radiance, which passed between her half-closed eyelids and from her stammering mouth with pearly teeth. The man's cupped hand imprisoned her breasts, his kisses fell at random, burning and passionate. Leaning further over the inert body, he had the sensation that the naked flesh was entering into him, with all its splendors and all its mysteries.

Exhausted by the effort he had made, by his anger and the anguish of his impotence, Starzo uttered a long cry, and let himself slide into the muddy water.

V

AT the muted splash, Ahassuru darted a suspicious glance around him, but he saw nothing except the immense rushes hiding banks of black and putrid mud, the exhalations of which were mortal. He gave an order to row vigorously, in order to escape the redoubtable zone.

Starzo's muted fall had caused all his flesh to shiver, and now there was a great silence, only interrupted by the sound of the oars. They drew away from the city in order to reach the dwelling of the satrap, in the low plain, bordered by the wood of torture, under the somber flight of vultures.

Ahassuru, the cruel tyrant, was not thinking about the millenary eras of suffering that the kings of Chaldea and Assyria had inflicted upon their peoples. The periodic uprisings, terminated in blood, and the frightful executions that overturned the land left him indifferent. Susiana, Babylonia, Phoenicia and Syria had been subjugated, in turn, by the likes of Sargon, Sennacherib and Assurbanipal. And everywhere, along the roads, enemies had writhed, crucified, flayed or quartered, whose lamentable bodies attracted innumerable birds of prey. The victors delivered themselves to bloody debaucheries, orgies of murder detailed subsequently on the walls of their palaces. Pyramids of severed human heads, feet and hands covered the ramparts, and long files of stakes extended as far as the eye could see over the sinister landscape.

But Ahassuru, the sanguinary satrap, enjoyed that spectacle, proud of the crimes he committed. Even the frail and touching beauty of his favorites did not retain him when they had ceased to please. The Euphrates carried away the secret of his amours in its troubled waters, and the public crier of Mylitta had already sold him many wives who had never been seen again. But Ahassuru paid a good price, and avaricious parents rarely resisted the temptation to confide their daughters to him.

The wall of the great palace, the entablature of which was ornamented with the heads of lions, suddenly appeared, looming up against the molten sky, and the satrap made a sign to the oarsmen to approach the bank.

The sumptuous dwelling could only be that of a princely family. An open portico projected from the wall, flanked by two immense bulls with human faces. Through the large bays between the columns, narrow openings were perceptible that served as windows. Above reigned a terraced roof of stone slabs. The heavy house of Ahassuru, standing up in the sand like a redoubtable monster, dominated the entire landscape with its equivocal slumber.

A long howl rose from the ditches. That was the chained prisoners, saluting the advent of the tyrant; their impotent anger made the plain vibrate.

Two men carried Ahmosis away with infinite precaution; unconscious, she remained inert in their arms.

"This way," said Ahassuru, swinging the heavy door of his dwelling. Two stout and lumpen eunuchs with flaccid flesh knelt down before him in order to receive his orders. Guards along the balustrades remained motionless and impassive, scarcely glancing at the amorous prey who passed before them in all the glory of her lilial beauty.

Then there was a rapid course through long corridors, halls with terrifying bas-reliefs and ceilings painted in bright colors. Long series of sculptures dressed the walls to a height of three meters, reproducing scenes of carnage, strange and complicated tortures, lion-hunts and merciless combats. A few brief legends in cuneiform inscriptions accompanied those cruel works and explained them, in chronological order.

"Here!" said the master, lifting a curtain.

They went into a high-ceilinged room surrounded by a green plinth. The walls were lined with enameled bricks representing blooming flowers with blue, yellow and white corollas. Svelte stems and gracious clumps of rare plants ran everywhere, making a contrast with the anguishing bas-reliefs of the other halls. A vast bed borne by ranks of captives, made of thuya wood imbricated with gold, occupied the center of a parquet made from sheets of brightly-colored glass.

"Lay her on the bed," said Ahassuru.

Then, when the young woman was offered to his desire like a fruit of flesh that his hand had not yet plucked, he dismissed the two men.

He placed his fingers on the slender legs, and moved them nervously all the way to the knees, as soft and fresh as two lotus petals. The proud curve of the hips arrested his gaze; he was about to unseal the closed pyx of the loins when the virgin uttered a profound sigh and suddenly sat up.

"Who are you?" she said, horrified.

He started like a wounded lion.

"I'm your master . . ."

"My master! I have no master. You've taken me away by force, without consulting my heart. I don't recognize your right to dispose of my person."

Her nostrils flared; her eyebrow drew together like ebony bows.

He thought he could vanquish her with promises.

"I'll give you necklaces of gold and cornelian," he said, "plaques of lapis lazuli, and emerald clasps. You'll have silver mirrors, perfumes, embroidered garments, veils, and slaves . . ."

The young woman smiled dolorously. "Yes," she said. "Give me something to hide my nudity."

She hoped thus to send the tyrant away, and perhaps to escape his odious desire, but he clutched her against him, gripping her long and supple figure, crushing her breasts against his rude leather-clad chest.

"I'll give you all my jewels," he said. "You'll be the most beautiful and most ornamented of my wives, but before then, I want your kiss, your caress. It's necessary to merit what I offer you. In any case, I could demand it, for I've paid a good price for you, and you're mine."

"No," she said. "You couldn't buy me from Morphy, who isn't my mother."

"Morphy took you in when you were little."

"Morphy stole me," said the young woman, proudly. "I know, by virtue of a fetish that was on my person, which I had worn for a long time, that I'm of illustrious birth."

Ahassuru burst out laughing. "Some magician's relic. Isn't old Morphy something of a diviner and sorceress?"

"I belong to a foreign race," Ahmosis went on, proudly. "I don't have your coppery tint, or your prominent cheekbones, or your oblique eyes. I have smooth hair and a straight nose; my skin is a clear brown, like that of the daughters of Egypt. I was born on the banks of the Nile, and I still retain the vision of large gardens bordered by mimosas and Pharaonic fig-trees, where my infancy was spent. In my dreams, I see bearded vultures passing overhead with shrill cries; I gaze at pink ibises asleep on one leg on the cornices of monuments, and slaves with glistening torsos, polished like basalt, bringing me fresh water in heavy jars."

"Truly, child," said the curious master, "you've seen all that?"

"Yes," she said. "I've seen a great palace with a pavilion flanked by two imposing wings. The staged galleries had columns mounted on lotus buds, and at the top, the flowers were in bloom. In the middle of the courtyard a jet of water murmured, and I loved to sit down on the edge of the basin in order to pluck the blue and pink corollas that floated on the crystalline water. All around me there were mimosas, tamarisks, pomegranates and acacias with embalmed clusters, and when I had chased mauve lizards over the brilliant stones, and golden scarabs in the heart of lilies. I listened to the song of sacred priestesses. It was one of them who taught me to play the Egyptian harp, much more sonorous than your crudely mounted short harps."

"You shall sing for me," said the master, laughing. "It also seems to me that I know your flowery palace. Perhaps the hazards of war have taken me into a dwelling similar to the one you've depicted for me; perhaps I dreamed it in the arms of a pretty daughter of your homeland."

"Let me go!" said Ahmosis, taking two steps toward the door.

But he retained her, a crease of hatred in the corners of his lips.

He thought that once his desire was satisfied, he would not keep this rebellious girl, whose pride had such annoying revolts. He would give her as fodder to wild beasts, or unleash his birds of prey upon her, trained to put out the eyes of prisoners. After the possession, the vengeance, more voluptuous still! And how preferable the sight of blood, sobs and death-rattles were to confessions, delirious kisses and ecstatic transports!

VI

HIMROUD, the satrap's latest wife, was becoming
bored in her high chamber, to which the plaints
of prisoners rose up night and day. She knew the language of all those accursed individuals, and sometimes,
leaning over the terrace that overhung the sinister
ditches, she spoke to the men awaiting death, sowing
hope and amour. In order to listen to her they fell silent,
trembling and tamed; on their knees in the fetid mud,
they lifted their fleshless hands, bruised by irons, toward
her. Their hideous and bloody heads were bathed by a
soft radiance, and their ecstatic eyes rediscovered tears.

"Save us! Save us!" they begged, incessantly.

And Himroud was desolate, for she was too paltry
to impose her will on the master.

That day she had seen Ahassuru return to the palace
with a new prey, and she thought that her reign was
over, that the executioners would soon come in search
of her, in order to subject her to a fate similar to that of
the prisoners.

Himroud was beautiful, however.

Under a heavy bundle of dark hair, she had a round face and long, impenetrably dark eyes that seemed to slide a moist caress between their immense lashes. She was made to be cherished by delirious hearts and fêted by words worthy of her splendor; but she was languishing sadly, already disdained, her only pleasure being the caresses of Myrr, the bird of prey, which she had been able to tame.

To please her, Myrr had renounced the feast of human eyeballs that his master offered him. Those delicate morsels now left him indifferent; he preferred a kiss from Himroud to bloody orgies. He remained for a long time perched on her shoulder or nestled on the young woman's knees, closing his yellow eyes in an intense bliss, while her caressant hand strayed over the bird's brown plumage.

She allowed her nostalgic mind to wander in distant reveries. She had an impotent desire to savor the mildness of her fictions indefinitely, and she gazed at the bleak course of the Euphrates, and the undermined trees in certain small arms of the river, the bared roots of which spread out over the ground. Humus formed a kind of exceedingly thin vegetal layer in places around the strong roots, covering the stagnant water with a rutilant verdure. Those muddy crusts opened up to imprudent individuals who ventured on to them an abyss of thick mire in which they became trapped, and the satrap often amused himself by plunging prisoners condemned to death neck-deep there.

If the young woman turned her eyes away from those marshes she perceived hideous grimacing heads nailed to the trees, partly eaten away already by the vultures, and her dream always fell back into cloacas of mud and blood.

Bordered by mangroves and black reeds, the river seemed, at that location, to absorb the glittering rays of the torrid sun without reflecting them. As uniform as a bronze mirror, the river allowed large clusters of nympheas to float at its edges, with their pink and white flowers, as fleshy as faces. Sometimes, slender snakes, patched with ocher and cinnabar, were coiled in the heart of a calyx, tightening their voluptuous knots in that warm and damp abode. Birds plucked them out in passing, rising into the air and uttering brief and strident cries.

Hibiscuses with scarlet corollas rose to great heights; snakeroots with flesh-colored umbels, manzanitas with red berries, buckthorn and agaves formed a morbidly scented vegetal girdle around the marshes, which intoxicated the recluse gently, numbing her to the point of forgetfulness.

It was not forbidden to her, however, to walk in a certain part of the walled garden. She often went down there, protected by the vigilant flight of the huge bird of prey, which followed her under the cool shade of the magnolias with broad white flowers, the tulip trees, the sassafras, the palm trees and the banana trees. There were verdant retreats there where the foliage of aristolochias, bignonias and grenadillas intersected, tangled in a thick mesh, shedding embalmed petals at the slightest breath of wind.

The disk of the sun, hidden by the treetops, cast torrents of light in the distance, respectful of the flowery nest where dolor was sheltered. Then dusk suddenly arrived. The sky remained blue, with russet and orange clouds, as if powdered with gold. Beneath those softly tinted bands, a straight, narrow ribbon of fire ran along the horizon, increasingly flamboyant as the glorious star descended toward it. The sensation of sadness became more profound for Himroud, penetrating her soul, her body and her entire being with a rare power.

If the newcomer pleased the master, the former wife, she knew, would be sacrificed. Perhaps that was only a question of days now, and perhaps of hours.

In reality Ahassuru was merely a heroic and cruel warrior. He only unleashed formidable and merciless war in hunts full of danger, in which he fought hand to hand with the enormous lions of the Chaldean solitudes.

His scribes, on returning from distant expeditions, recorded on tablets the number of severed heads and hands brought back with the enemy booty. Those heaps of human remains rotted in the sun, before the fearful eyes of prisoners thrown into the ditches to await the inevitable torture.

The Semites with hooked noses, thick lips and oblique eyes, gorged themselves on blood delightedly, and the satrap Ahassuru was no exception, in that time of crime and lust.

Nabuchodonosor,[1] surrounded by his chiefs, re-

---

1 I have retained the author's spelling—which occurs elsewhere in *fin-de-siècle* fiction, in which the king in question sometimes

mained the master and the measure of all things: the religion, life and death of his subjects. He remained the descendant of the formidable god Assur. In his name, he commanded military and civil forces, directed grim warriors and burned incense on sacrificial altars.

The vast empires of the likes of Assurbanipal and Nabuchodonosor were governed by satraps who called themselves "supreme masters," and among those proven chiefs Ahassuru had created a renown, famous for ferocity and bravery. There was nothing for which to hope from that sanguinary soldier, that grim male. Himroud knew that, so she awaited her condemnation with a bleak despair.

---

figured as a paradigm of aristocratic decadence—of the name of the individual more familiarly known in English as Nebuchadnezzar II, the king of Babylon from 605-562 B.C. When the present story was written the king in question was primarily known through Biblical references in the book of *Jeremiah* and the book of *Daniel*, although archeological evidence had already begun to suggest that both accounts of his reign are distorted, and that the latter text is entirely fictitious.

48

VII

WITH the exception of the clamor of the birds of prey, busy with some bloody task, everything fell silent; around the satrap's dwelling, all was quiet, calm, and motionless. There was not the slightest breath of wind to be felt, and yet the reeds of the marsh, which were visible from the terrace where Himroud was standing, were undulating gently, as if agitated by the passage of a crawling body.

A few frightened birds suddenly rose up in the middle of the rushes and skimmed the water, uttering cries of terror.

Interested, the young woman leaned over the stone sill and called softly to Myrr, the favorite hawk. But Myrr, who was hovering over the marsh, did not come in response to her voice, as he was accustomed to do. Something was definitely happening in the muddy water, which the plants prevented her from seeing.

"Myrr! Myrr!" the recluse called, again, looking down at the horrible ditch where the prisoners, overwhelmed by the heat of the day, were vaguely somnolent.

They were bound together in groups of four or five, and their bonds dug into their flesh, hollowing out wounds that bled incessantly. Starved, tortured and exhausted, they were waiting for the pittance that Himroud sometimes succeeded in stealing for them; but the odor that rose up from those charnel-houses, where the dead remained attached to the living, was so frightful that the young woman almost fainted in fulfilling her mission of pity.

The plants of the marsh had become motionless again, as if the hidden body crawling through them had suddenly stopped.

Surprised, her heartbeat increasing hopefully, Himroud waved her white veil above her head.

Then she thought that the movement of the aquatic plants might perhaps have been due to the passage of a wild animal, and that there was no reason to be excited by it. Sadly, she took a few steps in order to return to her room; but the branches suddenly parted, and a man dragging himself on his hands and knees soon appeared on the edge of the marsh.

Himroud immediately put a finger over her lips in order to recommend him to silence, and he replied with the same gesture of prudence as he returned to his damp shelter. The young woman waited anxiously for night, hoping to be able to speak to the mysterious visitor when the master and the slaves of Ahassuru's dwelling were asleep. At that time the guards relaxed their surveillance, knowing that the ditches were too deep and the bonds too solid to permit the prisoners to escape.

The day went by with its habitual monotony. The satrap, entirely devoted to his new amour, forgot himself with Ahmosis, in spite of the revolts and disdain of the young woman.

For her, slaves sang interminable chants softly, to a slow cadence; for her, nostalgic dancers went through their voluptuous paces. They were brown girls with violently made-up faces; their supple bodies undulated and folded, miming brutal amour in all its unconsciousness. They summoned desire by the arching of backs and lascivious torsion; they spurred the fantasy of the satrap, who, already drunk on wine and crime, loved their precise gestures.

It was a very material dance, in which woman was nothing more than amorous flesh, an instrument of pleasure of disquieting docility. It was automatic lust, devoid of soul and poetry.

Ahmosis had to submit to the passion of the master, who bent her weakness cruelly, and bruised her frail body, her slender arms and her delicate loins in frightful embraces. Then, finally left alone, she remained annihilated vaguely hypnotized, in the shade of the high-ceilinged room, listening to the almost imperceptible noise of a thin jet of water that murmured incessantly.

She thought about her mysterious infancy in the great Egyptian palace, and then her obscure existence in Babylon, to which she had been brought by old Morphy, the fortune-teller and maleficent sorceress.

That dated from the decisive campaign of Nabuchodonosor, who, after taking Jerusalem and having vanquished proud Tyr itself, had defeated the king of Egypt, Necho.[1] The Jews had followed the Chaldean army, trafficking children, and Morphy must have been among the number of those abductors.

Everything was blurred, however, in the girl's head; she could not make her distant memories precise. Alone with the old witch, eccentric and malevolent, she had found a friend and protector in the boatman Starzo. The young man often brought her pretty, iridescent fish with coral fins, and aquatic flowers with fleshy calices, whose bitter and intoxicating odor she loved. The nympheas reminded her of the amber incense-burners and the women of her homeland, fervently clasping blue, pink or white lotus flowers. Golden crocuses, safflowers and trichocereus cacti with red flowers formed sumptuous crowns for her, with which she ornamented her head, laughing, and the multicolored berries of the marshes, threaded artfully, constituted for her necklaces of cornelian, peridots and lapis lazuli.

In his rush baskets Starzo also brought her freshwater mussels, honey and sesame cakes, ruby pomegranates, topaz and amethyst grapes, and all the wild fruits that he collected at random during his long excursions between the shady banks.

"Starzo," she said, caressing the young man with her small hands, "I love you very much, and I'd like to live with you forever. You're good and generous; you only ever have kind words; one can see your soul in your eyes . . ."

---

1 Necho II was king of Egypt from 610-595 B.C. He was defeated in battle by Nebuchadnezzar II, but the latter's capture of Jerusalem is nowadays dated to 587 B.C., some years after Necho's death.

"Mistress," he said, ecstatically. "Glorious little star!"

"Yes, yes, you're all that I cherish in the world, for nowhere else have I found divine pity, forbearance and devotion. Morphy only has wounding words for me, insults and blows. I have to serve her like a slave, dance in front of people to earn her money, or sing, accompanying myself on my Egyptian harp. Sometimes, when her spells haven't brought her anything, she even makes me beg along the streets or in front of the temples of Mylitta. I hate her, you see, and her death would make me happy!"

Starzo took the child on his knees, passing his tremulous fingers through her warm, silky and electric hair.

"Would you like to be my wife, little Ahmosis?"

"I'd like that," she said, emotional with gratitude for the humble companion of her games and her poverty.

In reality, she was ignorant of amour, but her being was full of an immense affection.

As for Starzo, he adored the brown child with the cameo profile, and the eyes full of dreams and tenderness.

"Will you love me as I love you?" he repeated, anxiously. "I'm very little for a girl as pretty as you."

"What more could I want?"

"I don't know. But you'll be sold in the temple of the goddess; your beauty might be noticed by a powerful lord."

"I'd refuse to belong to him."

"You won't have the right to do that, alas, for the will of virgins isn't consulted."

But she had laughed, amused by her friend's fears. "It's necessary, between now and then, my dear Starzo, to amass a fortune, in order to pay dearly for me at the auction of Mylitta."

He sighed bitterly. "I earn so little in my profession of boatman. I'll never be rich enough to pay what you're worth."

"I'll make myself ugly, you'll see!"

"The connoisseurs won't be deceived."

"I'll bruise myself all over. I'll cut off my hair and eyelashes.

"No, no, I forbid you to do that!" he cried, angered by the idea of such a sacrifice.

She consoled him quickly. "What's the point in tormenting yourself, my dear Starzo. Many things might happen before I'm of an age to be sold."

And now, without waiting for that age, Morphy had dragged her to the market of virgins in spite of her plaints and revolts. No one had listened to her, no one had defended her, and now she was the wife of Ahassuru, the detested satrap.

Ahmosis thought about her friend, whom she had seen disappearing into the morbid rushes, and who might already be nothing more than a cadaver torn apart by birds of prey, wolves and jackals.

Tears streamed over the young woman's cheeks; she dug her fingernails into her breasts, and then fell back into a bleak prostration.

VIII

THE curtain that masked the entrance to her room was slowly raised, however; a woman paused indecisively on the threshold.

Her body was covered by a gauze tunic, without veiling her any more than the pure water of a spring veils the body of a bather. Large golden disks trembled on her cheeks; and an enamel and pearl gorgerin sustained her breasts.

"Who are you?" asked Ahmosis, surprised.

"I'm Himroud, the satrap's wife."

"The first wife of Ahussuru?"

"The one who is doubtless about to die, for the tyrant causes the women who have ceased to please him to disappear. Many unfortunates before me have had the same fate."

"I'd rather disappear than live in such a painful subjection. Would you like to take my place and tell me how I can get out of here?"

"Alas, the exits are guarded; you wouldn't get far," Himroud sighed.

"Then let's die together. This existence horrifies me."

"Listen," said the young woman. "A man is hiding in the marsh. I made him a sign to wait for night in order to slip as far as the terrace of my room."

Ahmosis' heart began to beat violently. "Oh!" she said. "Starzo isn't dead! He alone could brave all dangers to reach us!"

"Starzo?"

"Yes, my friend, my fiancé. I'll tell you later everything that he's done for me already. Nothing is lost, since Starzo is alive!"

"Nothing is lost," repeated Himroud, joyfully.

"You knew, then, that I wanted to flee?" said Ahmosis, surprised.

"I knew from the slaves that you wept all day long and refused the master's caresses. I knew that you'd been brought here like a breathless prey and that a rape had occurred between the walls of this accursed chamber. So many others before you have suffered the same fate!"

"You did well to come," said the girl. "Two of us will be cleverer and stronger. What do you want to do?"

"I don't know yet."

"Starzo will advise us. You'll see him and talk to him tonight? Try not to attract the attention of the guards."

"They often drink and play dice while the master is asleep. I'll wait for that moment."

Ahmosis and Himroud looked at one another curiously. They were both beautiful, although dissimilar. Amber and gold reflections colored the ardent pallor of the girl, and her long dark eyes with arched eyebrows had a singular expression in her dainty, almost infantile face. She was smiling now, for a smile was the habitual expression of that fleshy mouth with the mutinous lips. Her short hair, cut squarely, in the Egyptian fashion, stood out slightly to either side of her pure cheeks; she was full of juvenile grace, elegant and frail.

Himroud was paler than Ahmosis, but her forms were less delicate; she showed a glorious and supple body, with firm breasts and powerful loins. Pendants were quivering in her ears; necklaces of amber, cornelian and peridot, ornamented with little silver plaques and fetishes, surrounded her round and polished neck. She had the beauty of Chaldean women, more blooming and more robust than that of frail Egyptian statuettes.

"Tonight!" repeated Ahmosis. "Oh, how I long for tomorrow. But how will I know what Starzo has said to you?"

"After the satrap's visit, come to my chamber."

"Your chamber?"

"Yes, it's at the end of this gallery; I'll leave the doors open. It's better not to admit the slaves to the confidence of our projects. Send them away on some pretext."

"Oh," said Ahmosis, "I'm almost always alone, for the maladroit cares of those women are painful for me. I sent them away from the outset."

"That's good," said Himroud. "May the peace of the gods be with you."

"May your life be long and full!"

They smiled at one another and embraced; then Himroud drew away slowly, gliding through the shadows like a great golden serpent, undulating slowly.

IX

THE stone lions and the monstrous winged bulls extended their paws, raising their heads in the warm and transparent night. Everything was silvery in the moonlight, interrupted here and there by blue-tinted clumps of bushes. The stars were blinking their long mysterious eyelashes in the violet firmament, gilded by infinite stardust.

Himroud now had an imperious need to act, prove the reality of her energy, for she did not doubt that, with the collaboration of this Starzo about whom Ahmosis had talked to her, everything could be arranged in accordance with her desires. She was meditating an entire escape plan in the discreet and protective night. Thoughts rolled in tumultuous waves in her head, while her eyes were fixed on the motionless reeds of the marsh, awaiting the appearance of the boatman.

But Starzo did not show himself. Perhaps he had gone to sleep in the unhealthy plants, amid the mortal exhalations of those decomposed waters? Perhaps he had been devoured by the wild beasts that the satrap kept in his gardens to serve for the torture of prisoners? Trees leaning over the bank had the appearance of terrible grim giants in the moonlight. They were fantastically twisted, stretching out their long arms as if to seize invisible prey.

That pool of stagnant water was identified with the young woman's dreams to such an extent that she found the color of her soul therein. Sitting on the terrace of the sinister palace for long hours, she let her gaze wander over the glaucous vegetation, searching there for the explanation of her futile existence. She saw magic spells and presages in the tremulous silken surfaces, in the pale glimmers and the mists that floated over the marsh like delicate muslins, sometimes veiling the mask of the moon.

At present, the immobility of the rushes and branches frightened her. She interrogated the darkness with an increasing anguish. That dormant water, lying in its secret bed, attracted and killed its imprudent lovers. A slow and maleficent force, it wrapped its fluid coils around in soft embraces, and did not let go of its victims.

A pink lizard running past the young woman made her tremble suddenly. She thought she had seen a hand advancing from the darkness to seize her. Green and blue flies swirled around her, and suddenly, the plaint of the prisoners erupted in the ditches beneath the terrace.

Himroud showed herself then, in order to impose silence on the unfortunates, to try to make them understand that a favorable event was doubtless about to dispose of their fate.

Their heads were raised toward her pale silhouette, and their groans gradually died away in a profound sigh.

At the same moment, a man, parting the tall vegetation, appeared near the marsh. He took a few cautious steps; then, lying down in the sand, he crawled to the edge of the ditch.

"I was waiting for you," said Himroud. "Are you not Starzo, the boatman?"

The young man stifled a cry of joy. "It's Ahmosis who told you? She thought that I'd be able to find her?"

"Yes, she had confidence in your amour and your courage."

"Let her come," he begged. "Tell her to come on to the terrace for a moment. I don't know you, but you must be good, since she's chosen to open her heart to you."

"Alas," said Himroud, "Ahmosis is secluded. However, you'll see her soon. You'll save us all, for you're brave . . ."

"What is it necessary to do?"

"See those men who are agonizing beneath you? They're doomed to certain death, because they're prisoners of war. Their bonds are solid, the ditch is deep. Find a means of freeing them."

"I'll find one," said Starzo, confidently. "Their aid will, in fact, be a great help to us."

"Be prudent!" Himroud whispered, having just heard a slight sound. "Go away, and I'll see you at the same time tomorrow."

Crawling, the young man regained the tall vegetation of the marsh, in which he hid, invisible to everyone, even the alert gaze of his accomplice. The formidable guards, bearing smoky torches, appeared along the terraces, soldiers lined up in their immobile ranks, bucklers on their thighs, maces in one hand and spears in the other.

Himrod went back into her room, with a confident smile at the corners of her lips and a glimmer of hope in her dark eyes.

X

THE master has quit his new wife after the brutal embrace, the kiss as grim as a bite. It has been an hour of terrible amour, from which she has emerged bruised, degraded, and ready for any crime. The melancholy sound of instruments is cradling her misery; harps are weeping in pearly chords and nostalgic voices uniting in those singular chants made of sighs and sobs.

Without even repairing the disorder of her veils, Ahmosis has headed for Himroud's chamber, following the indications she has given her.

The sated satrap will not come again to menace her with his odious caresses; she is free for some time, and she is in haste to have news of Starzo.

Himroud is waiting for her in her most beautiful adornments. She has put tubular pearls and coral beads in her blue-tinted hair. A gold band circles her forehead, accompanying the roses of her temples; her ear-plaques have pendants of onyx, garnet and emerald. Rows of jasper, lapis and carnelian sheathe her neck; amulets hang down over her naked breasts with rigid tips.

"I was waiting for you, little Ahmosis, and I'm glad to see you."

"By the gleam in your eyes and the joy in your smile, I divine, Himroud, that you have good news to give me?"

The two women embraced, giving one another a kiss of alliance.

"I've seen Starzo," said Himroud.

"Starzo! It's really him!"

"He'll free us all."

"Oh! I knew that I could count on him."

"He's brave, and he adores you."

"Then we'll be leaving soon? I'm in haste to shrug off the odious yoke."

But the young woman sighed. "It might be necessary to be patient, for there are great difficulties."

"That's true," said Ahmosis, suddenly somber. "The guards watch day and night. What can a poor boatman do against such a redoubtable force?"

"Another force, even more terrible, is waiting in the shadows. That's the one I'm counting on, most of all."

"Another force?"

"Yes—look."

Himroud drew the girl on to the terrace and showed her the prisoners chained up in the horrible deep ditch.

But Ahmosis uttered a dejected plaint. "A frightful vision!" she said, retreating swiftly. "Those men are covered in blood, their arms are bruised by the ropes. They'll never have enough energy to escape!"

"Starzo will liberate them, be certain of it. Anger and the desire for vengeance will give those wretches an artificial energy. Let's have confidence..."

"Yes, console me. I'm devoid of strength and will."

"Let's forget the peril."

"How?"

"Here's my harp. Would you like to try it, little Ahmosis?"

"My fingers are trembling like leaves; I'd only be able to make the sonorous strings groan. Play, you who are able to maintain a radiant forehead in the midst of ordeals."

The young woman drew nearer to the terrace, in order to send the captives the echo of her hopes and lull their misery by means of a song of amour.

And her melodious dream rose up, symbolic of a mysterious but magical joy. That delight went toward the painted statue of a god of bounty and tenderness, toward an unknown being, long anticipated, a divine, suave and marvelous lover. Her intoxication lost itself in something unknown and knowable, which had to have an extreme gentleness.

Himroud's voice was warm and charming; her supple fingers seemed to fly over the strings like tame birds.

But Ahmosis, jealous, wanted to play in her turn.

"Sing," she said. "I'll follow your improvisation, and we'll associate our chimeras."

"Yes," said Himroud, "we'll mingle our passionate desires, and that will be better."

"I know the prestigious songs of Egypt."

"I know the Chaldean songs of war."

"I can express all the real poetry of the caress."

"I can render all the somber horror of carnage."

"My voice has the tender softness of the plaint of a turtle-dove."

"My voice has the amplitude of a warrior hymn."

"I shall speak of sensuality."

"And I of vengeance."

"Let's begin," said Ahmosis, running her tapering fingers over the strings of the great instrument of eloquent harmonies.

And Himroud's voice rose up, broad and vibrant, speaking of merciless combats and the ardent felicity of vengeance. It was as harsh and tearing as the clamor of a hurricane, as dolorous and profound as the plaint of the sea breaking over rocks.

Then Ahmosis sang in her turn, for Starzo the boatman, who ought to be listening on the edge of the glaucous marsh. And to be sure, he remained ecstatic in the supple reeds, under the flight of dragonflies with glassy, nacreous and quivering wings, larger than hummingbirds. On the edge of the pool, the undulating vegetation tightened its grip; he was able to believe, while closing his eyes, that his beloved was beside him, stroking him, as she had done before on the quays of Babylon.

XI

STARZO could swim like a fish. After his brief faint he had come round at the surface of the water, and had continued to follow the boat that was carrying Ahmosis away at a distance.

In any case, he knew where the satrap lived, having often sailed that far in order to collect aquatic flowers, lanceolate ferns, and the gold and crimson seeds that he gave the young girl. He even pushed on as far as the asphalt springs whose long black streams snaked in a sinister fashion over the blonde surface of the sands to lose themselves in the river.

The boatman had explored some parts of the hot arid region that extends from the plateau of Iran all the way to the shores of the Mediterranean. He had seen long caravans come from Sidon and Tyre all the way to Babylon. He had crossed the path of Ethiopian boats laden with precious materials going up the course of the Tigris and the Euphrates in order to trade in fabrics, perfumes and precious stones.

All the glaucous pools in the forests of reeds were familiar to him, for it was in the aquatic flora that he made his most astonishing discoveries.

Even the pestilential exhalations of the marshes did not cause him any malaise, and his primitive boat circulated between the long supple stems that sometimes grew to a height of four or five meters.

The shallow depths of the Euphrates opposed the progress of large boats, and everywhere that digging channels had not been attempted, only light skiffs could pass, visiting the little arms of the river, which usually terminated is marshes.

Rain, says Herodotus, *is not frequent in Chaldea. The little water that falls develops the roots of sown grains. Then the plants are irrigated with river water, which enables them to reach maturity. It is not the same as in Egypt, where the river spreads out of its own accord into the surrounding area. It is only by means of its arms or with the aid of machinery that irrigation takes place. In addition, Babylonia, like Egypt, is entirely cut by canals, the largest of which can carry ships. It heads south-westwards from the Euphrates to the Tigris, on which Nineveh is situated. Of all the countries we know, it is certainly the best and most fertile in the fruits of Ceres. No one tries to make the soil produce figs, vines or olives, but in compensation, it is appropriate to all kinds of grains; it always produces two hundred times as much as is sown, and in the years when it surpasses itself it renders three hundred times as much as it has received. The leaves of wheat and barley are four fingers broad there. Although I am not unaware of the height to which stems of millet and sesame grow, I shall make no mention of it, convinced that those who have not been to Babylonia will not be able to believe what I have reported about the grains of that land.*

The Babylonians do not make use of olive oil, but that of sesame. The plain is covered by palm trees. The majority bear fruit; only a part of it is eaten, and wine and honey are extracted from the rest.

In his primitive boat, Starzo pierced the blue arches of the watery roads that tall enlaced plants with bitter scents sometimes form, endlessly. The fleshy flowers with ardent pistils intoxicated him delightfully. He loved the magic of the water and the passionately confounded plants. He also listened to their wordless music, which went to the soul like a kind of harmonious spell, exquisite and perfidious.

Between the soft reeds, the water murmured the name of his beloved to him; emerald fingers and fingernails caressed him in passing; pink grasses sprinkled him with an embalmed dust. And all those flowers and all that foliage, swollen with water, cradled him between their fervent garlands during the most oppressive hours of the day.

The boatman knew the satrap's somber dwelling, surrounded by the wood of tortures, stakes lined up in sinister avenues of nightmare and murder.

That place was the favorite abode of birds of prey, which had bloody orgies there, for Ahassuru made war incessantly, always bringing back more prisoners.

Starzo had seen the master reenter his dwelling with the dearly beloved carried by the oarsmen. He had heard the heavy door close on the young woman, and when night fell he had slipped into the marshes bordering the gardens.

The verdant bed of the banks was familiar to him. He had slept there, nourishing himself on berries and aquatic plants, awaiting a propitious moment to show himself and act. The gods, he thought, would not abandon him in his perilous mission, and he prayed in particular for Mylitta, the lady of love and sensuality, to be favorable to him.

The wild beasts in the gardens scented him in passing, the muscles of their backs tensing under the warm skin, the fur bristling with fear or surprise, but they soon drew away indifferently, in the expectation of other feasts.

XII

ON the second day, Starzo had seen Himroud leaning over the terrace; then he had heard the mild words that she had addressed to the captives, and had said to himself that the compassionate woman would certainly be a useful ally.

On the third day he had shown himself, and everything had been accomplished in accordance with his desire. Now he was forming an escape plan. With supple and solid creepers he knotted ladders, counting on descending by that means into the deep ditches. He would break the chains of the first prisoners, who would then liberate their companions and emerge from the filthy sepulcher.

When night had fallen he advanced, crawling toward the terrace, as he had done before.

"Courage," he said. "Have confidence, and be alert."

"Is the moment of deliverance imminent, then?" asked Himroud, whose heart was beating tumultuously.

"Perhaps."

"And how will you do it?"

"Don't ask me for my secret; I even fear confiding it to the trees. In any case, you'll see me at work and you'll understand. Be ready, as well as Ahmosis, for it will be necessary to obey me with docility."

"We'll obey you, Starzo, whatever you decide."

After a moment of ardent hesitation, the young man asked: "But won't I be able to see her? Her presence would give me so much courage,"

"The master is with her," said Himroud. "Tomorrow you'll see her, for the satrap is due to leave on a warrior expedition. You'll see her, I promise you, and we'll act . . ."

"We'll act," said Starzo, vibrant with hatred.

"Go now; it's necessary that no one suspects your presence; we'd be doomed."

"Until tomorrow," said the young man, in a whisper.

"Until tomorrow."

The prisoners were listening anxiously. They too had understood; a glimmer of hope traversed their anguished souls.

In the hottest hour of the day, Ahmosis came, as she had the day before, to visit her new friend. She had put on her pink coral hood, the pearls of which trembled over her cheeks, and had ornamented herself with the satrap's jewels.

"Have you seen Starzo?" she asked, when she had returned the young woman's affectionate kiss.

"He came while the guards were asleep on the terraces. He'll act soon, be certain of it."

"He told you so?"

"Yes, but I don't know his plans. I only know that the satrap is going away to make war and we won't be watched as closely."

Ahmosis clapped her little hands joyfully. "The master's going away! Oh, what luck. Doubtless he'll take all his soldiers?"

"The eunuchs and the slaves will remain, with part of the militia . . ."

"And how will we get away?"

"I don't know, but Starzo will warn us when the time comes."

"My handsome Starzo! Will I be able to see him?"

"When the master has gone; now it would be imprudent."

But Ahmosis uttered a cry of fright. Myrr, the large hawk, had just alighted on Himroud's arm, and was contemplating her amorously with his golden eyes.

"This is Myrr," said the young woman. "He's tame, and won't do you any harm. See how dainty he is!"

She caressed the tawny plumage of the bird, presenting him with a finger, which he pecked gently, his eyelids half-closed, in an ecstatic bliss.

"Would you like to stroke him in your turn? Here, Myrr is my only friend; in order to please me he has renounced feasting on human flesh, and he takes his meals with me, very sagely."

Ahmosis became a little girl again, forgetting the suffering of recent days, the physical and mental tortures. She had taken the large bird on to her knees and was teasing him, laughing.

"He'll be our companion in play later, when we've fled this horrible dwelling."

"He'll certainly follow us," said Himroud, thoughtfully. "When I walk in the part of the garden reserved for me, he hovers incessantly above my head; he's joyful when I'm joyful, and sad when I'm sad. He certainly understands me like a reasonable person, and I love to confide my daydreams to him."

Myrr allowed himself to be caressed by Ahmosis, half-closing his round eyes, which had imprisoned the sun's rays. His feet were velvet, like those of cats that have retracted their claws, and his wings were quivering happily.

"Here," said Himroud, "the animals are my friends. To them alone I open my heart, and tell them my troubles, for I know they won't betray me. Even the lions that wander in the garden night and day follow me meekly and rub themselves against my knees in a desire for affection. No animal is hostile to me, and I protect them all as much as I can."

"You're right," said Ahmosis. "I too like those obscure brothers, so superior to humans in their sentiments of devotion, gratitude and fidelity. Myrr will be as much my friend as yours."

"Adieu, little Ahmosis; it's necessary for us to separate."

"Already!"

The girl lifted up the bird, which seemed to have gone to sleep on her knees, and rendered it liberty. Opening his large tawny wings, Myrr traversed the terrace and disappeared into the tall vegetation of the marsh.

"He'll go to carry your caresses and your kisses to Starzo," said Himroud, laughing. "He's understood everything, you see."

"Oh, let the hour of liberty come soon! To flee, flee from this frightful place!" said Ahmosis, extending her arms toward the turquoise sky, a square of which she could perceive through the open door. "I no longer have anything but that ardent desire!"

She resumed the route to her room slowly, somewhat consoled by Himroud's promises, and slightly warmed by the sweetness of her amity.

XIII

A HASSURU was making preparations for his departure. The hope of prey magnetized that violent and grim soul. Projects of conquest and extermination were brooding within it. It was uplifted by visions of massacre and torture, dreaming of changing the waters of the Euphrates into waves of blood in order to frighten the people.

The satrap contemplated the bas-reliefs of his dwelling, which represented him triumphant everywhere, driving his war chariot over cadavers, slicing off hands and feet, and putting out the eyes of the vanquished with the point of his dagger.

The cohorts were moving off on the far side of the river, plunging into the bleak solitudes, following Nabuchodonosor, the voluptuous tyrant who, according to Judaic tradition, was condemned for his pride to become similar to the beasts and browse the grass in the fields.

The monarch was then in all his glory, and his magnificence was only equaled by that of lascivious and cruel satraps. He had subjugated Susiana, Armenia,

Phoenicia, Syria and northern Arabia; and when populations tried to rise up against his iron yoke the ever-ready chiefs fell upon the rebels, delivering themselves delightedly to bloody debauches and orgies of crime surely unique in human history.

A gallery in Ahassuru's palace displayed walls entirely covered by the skin of officers flayed alive. Cornices were formed by human skulls aligned in serried ranks. Tibias, femurs, humeri and radii framed complicated arabesques made with the phalanges of hands and feet, all sparkling like ivory. The cadavers of vanquished chiefs had furnished the elements of that sinister décor; large urns similar to the Egyptians' canopic jars contained the hearts of famous warriors.

Ahassuru was proud of those trophies and the thousands of less illustrious remains that were near his dwelling, for many decisive battles had been fought in that place. As soon as the devouring activity of the satrap relaxed, coalitions formed everywhere and revolts burst forth. It was therefore necessary to fight, and fight incessantly, to maintain the prestige of the army and the power of Babylon.

Ahassuru had made war on the king of Juda; then he had descended into Egypt in order to pitch his tents before Pelusium. It did not displease him to rediscover in the delicate features of Ahmosis, his new wife, the charming type of the country that he had conquered. Thus, his amour was redoubled by a certain perverse pleasure that he savored in the humiliation of the woman.

The satrap had tightened around his loins a large belt of crocodile skin; the clarions and the drums resounded with a din that caused vultures troubled in their sleep to take flight. The hoofbeats of horses, the thunder of bronze-rimmed wheels and the rattling of weapons accompanied the warrior hymn giving the signal for departure.

Sarazy-Pal, the chief of the eunuchs, was waiting respectfully for his lord's orders.

"Keep a good guard," said the satrap. "I haven't had time to execute the prisoners, but you can take charge of that concern."

"Your instruction will be carried out. Live forever, incomparable master!"

"Also watch over my slaves, over Himroud and Ahmosis. Do not allow them to leave the part of the garden reserved for them on any pretext."

"They will not go out."

"If either one of them rebels, you may act as I would act myself."

"I understand," said the eunuch, with a somber smile.

Satisfied, Ahassuru joined Nabuchodonosor's army. The satraps were reunited with the king in that fashion all along the route. Helmets, shields, scale armor and bronze blades glittered beneath the implacable sun. The chariots were succeeded by the battalions of the infantry, provided with bucklers, slings, axes, bows or spears. The formidable mass of warriors advanced like a hurricane, sweeping away everything in its passage, and the gods seemed to protect the sanguinary tyrants who only reigned in order to destroy more effectively.

XIV

"I'M dying of terror," said Ahmosis, penetrating into Himroud's chamber.

"What do you fear, since the master has gone?"

"I fear Sarazy-Pal."

"The chief eunuch? What has he done to you?"

"He's more redoubtable than the satrap; he has determined my death in order not to have to watch over me any longer. He certainly suspects something; he's going to kill me soon, and he's going to kill the captives contained in the ditches. They'll be executed tomorrow before the terraces."

"Who told you that?"

"The slaves."

"It's necessary to act, then," said Himroud, pensively. "As long as Starzo has completed the preparations for our flight!"

"Can't you talk to him?"

"I'll try."

The young woman advanced on to the terrace and her anxious gaze explored the surrounding area.

Everything seemed peaceful. Only the plaints of the

prisoners sometimes rose up in the silence, along with the clamor of the birds of prey.

On the edge of the marsh there was a movement in the reeds.

"Starzo has seen me," said Himroud. "He's coming."

"Can I show myself alongside you?" asked Ahmosis, trembling.

"Yes; that will give your friend courage; he'll be glad of your presence."

The two women leaned over the stone balustrade, and their contrasting beauty was illuminated by the sun's fiery radiance.

"Starzo, I love you!" said Ahmosis, with her lips rather than her voice. And with both hands, she sent a kiss to the young man.

"Tonight," said the boatman, "we'll leave."

"Everything is ready?" asked Himroud, joyfully.

"Yes. First I'll go down into the ditches to free the men who are tied up there. I've made a long ladder with creepers that will permit me to reach them."

"But the eunuch will be on watch and will raise the alarm."

"Try to put him to sleep."

"How?"

"I don't know. Find a means."

"Oh," said Himroud, "it's necessary to get him drunk. Sarazy-Pail likes palm wine. We'll be able to lure him with dourah and honey cakes, for he's greedy too."

"If he wants my jewels, I'll give them to him," added Ahmosis. "He must desire ingots of precious metal, for he's as avaricious as all eunuchs."

"Perhaps; but the offer of your jewelry might surprise him. Remember that in the satrap's absence he has the power of life and death over us. He certainly covets your enamel gorgerins and bracelets, and our necklaces of jasper, agate, sardonyx and onyx, but he knows that he can take them all without consulting us. He's already caused Monny, Serosys and Sagar, Ahassuru's first wives, to disappear; one murder more wouldn't cost him anything."

"Yes, yes, you're right; it's necessary to forestall his criminal projects; tomorrow it might be too late."

"Let me do it," said Himroud. "Everything will happen as we wish."

As soon as Starzo had returned to his hiding-place in the reeds, the two woman summoned slaves and ordered date-wine, palm wine and that of vines; liqueurs the color of amethyst, ruby and topaz; honey and sesame cakes, spicy pâtés and delicacies of every sort. Then they waited for dusk, exchanging their impressions and their dreads in low voices.

Everything seemed to be asleep in the vast dwelling. The air was replete with heavy perfumes of flowers and corruption: the powerful odors of the marsh and the charnel-house; the odors of acacia and tuberoses, lilies and vervain; redoubtable and delectable odors, brutally mixed, which made the heart leap. The sun spread a penetrating light that resembled a hot and motionless rain, a rain of precious stones on the silvery sand. Near the clumps of bushes, on the lawns, the huge lions, sated, were sleeping heavily . . .

Then, in the peace of things, the satrap's wife prostrated herself and implored the gods to be favorable to her.

XV

WHEN night had fallen, Himroud and Ahmosis adorned themselves as if for a fête; then they assembled the slaves and the eunuchs around them, and invited them to drink to the success of the satrap.

"May our prayers accompany the satrap and may he live forever," said Sarazy-Pal, with a mysterious smile.

"May he live forever," the women repeated, prostrate in an attitude of adoration and submission.

"Ahassuru has fully merited the honor of the gods and men," said Himroud, raising her cup filled with a golden liquid. "Tell us, Sarazy, about the conquests of the valorous chief. Have you seen all the executions, all the massacres and all the tortures of the vanquished warriors?"

"I have seen them."

"You can instruct us better than anyone else?"

Flattered, the eunuch swelled with pride, and commenced in a piercing nasal voice an interminable recitation of the satrap's crimes. The ecstatic slaves listened ardently, quivering at the cruelest vengeances. The two wives swooned with admiration, encouraging the narrator by means of numerous swigs of topaz-colored wine, a honeyed and fiery liquor.

"Let's drink!" said Ahmosis to Sarazy-Pal, the chief eunuch. And she lifted the cup to his lips with a charming laugh.

"Let's drink!" repeated Himroud, sending round the peppers and vehemently spiced cakes, and the delicacies with piquant and sugary flavors.

The eunuch, already drunk, related, while laughing, the exploits of the unchained human beast, the victims he had tortured, the ever-more-numerous murders, and the atrocities of the frightful orgies that followed those murders. Women danced, casually, vivaciously, lightly and lasciviously. Instruments purred under feverish hands; voluptuous clamors emerged from naked throats, and amphorae of clay, glass or metal circulated endlessly to the chords of harps and lyres and the warbling of double reed flutes, the moans of confused voices speaking hatred and amour simultaneously.

"Oh," Sarazy-Pal went on, his speech slurring, "enemies have often advanced on Babylon. They were disorderly bands of kings and haphazard warriors united in the same desire for victory. Egyptians. Libyans and Syrians have been repelled by our invincible troops. The satrap, our master, has always given the example of the most ardent bravery—and after his victories, what beautiful ceremonies of death!"

"You love him, then, your redoubtable lord?" asked Himroud.

"Certainly, for he doesn't refuse me anything. I'm well-treated here. I have precious fabrics, jewels and weapons, and the surveillance isn't difficult."

The guests are now sitting or lying around little tables laden with foodstuffs; a few women, unused to heady wines, have fallen asleep. Nudities are displayed in the vast room at the hazard of the orgy. The two wives are grouped with Sarazy, still upright, exciting him to drink with gestures and voices, and also drinking, in order to set an example, large cupfuls of luminous wine, which they throw over their shoulders.

A confused rumor informs them that the captives are agitated, perhaps liberated and preparing for the assault. They redouble their efforts in regard to the hideous eunuch, now sprawling on cushions. Ahmosis, lying on a porphyry step, simulates drunkenness; Himroud is singing a monotonous and barbaric Chaldean hymn in a hoarse voice.

The orgy becomes increasingly ardent, ablaze in a great flight of ignited desires. Two young girls with forms of an infinite delicacy, with slim waists beneath scarcely-flowered breasts, clasp one another in an embrace with cries of delight. A tall brunette young woman with blazing eyes and eyebrows joined by a harsh line, rushes a rival and plants a dagger in her loins. Others laugh, and others weep, unconscious, moved to compassion or fury.

"It's because we have nothing to refuse you," says a little girl, kissing the eunuch's bald head.

"You're handsome—almost as handsome as the master," says another, laughing. "With you, we have nothing to dread."

"Today, you're our lord!"

"Choose a companion at your whim!"

"Take two!"

"Take three!"

"Take us all!"

Sarazy-Pal, laughing blissfully, uncovers his black teeth and bloody gums. He is even more horrible in the expansion of his joy, and his enormous belly is making abrupt somersaults.

But a eunuch of the guard has entered at a run,

"The prisoners are loose! They're emerging from the ditches and breaking down the doors."

The guests, completely drunk, scarcely comprehend.

The frightened man resumes, with grand gestures: "We're going to be massacred. We're outnumbered! Can you hear the furious blows of the insurgents? The first door has already been smashed to smithereens."

Sarazy, his eyelids half-closed, utters ever more feeble gurgles. His head nods slackly, and then tips back into a hollow of the cushion, and a sonorous snore proves that nothing in the world will any longer be able to make him stir.

XVI

STARZO had waited for Himroud's signal before going into action. His ladder of creepers was all ready. It only remained to secure it solidly to the edge of a ditch.

By virtue of an overflow of the Euphrates, the captives had water up to their waists; since the previous day they had not ceased to moan, raising their sanguinary gaze toward the vaguely-shining narrow strip of sky. But a voice reached them; a man, clinging to a florid hank, a long rope of foliage, descended into the frightful gehenna in order to encourage them, perhaps to save them.

They listened to the generous speech, quivering with hope; they agitated in the fetid mud, drawing closer in order to be aided more rapidly. Bonds attached them by the neck, the feet and the arms, short enough to paralyze their movements, but Starzo was robust; he had sharpened weapons, and he succeeded in breaking the shackles of a few men, who liberated their companions in their turn.

Now there was the emergence, one by one, of those wretched skeletal forms with frightful, bloody heads, corroded eyelids and blue-tinted lips.

The boatman sustained them, pushed them toward the sheet of violet sky dotted with stars, and they arrived in the open air, tottering and weaker than children. A few laughed convulsively; others embraced their savior with tears of gratitude.

But Starzo drew himself up to his full height.

"It's necessary to act," he said, "to force the satrap's dwelling, to surprise and massacre the guards and the eunuchs, to take the women to Babylon, where revolt is growling and where pariahs can easily hide while awaiting the imminent revolution. The adventure will soon become monstrous and tragic; in the accursed palace, blood will mingle with the drunkenness of the feasting, the winy song of demented guests, and death-rattles. The dead will be thrown to the lions, and we'll flee without anxiety."

"We're with you," said the captives, who were rushing the doors. "Order, and we'll obey."

They all attacked at the same time, rediscovering strength in order to crush the enemy, to avenge their homeland and their brethren.

The guards, too few in number, resisted in vain. The assailants, taking their weapons, struck them furiously. Ten or twenty against one, they killed incessantly, grim, hideous and invincible. In the hall of the feast, while the most enraged took possession of Sarazy-Pal in order to torture him, the others threw themselves on the food and the women, equally avid for nourishment and amour.

All of them had come through the doors of the palace, furious, indomitable, unleashed beasts, and the great hall was red with spilled blood. The walls were red, as well as the table, the cushions, the paving-stones and the bodies lying in puddles of wine and perfume. Maddened by murder and desire, the men roared like wild beasts and fell upon their victims, sometimes killing them before possessing them. Strident screams, sobs and gasps frightened the great placid lions outside, and the birds of prey, which fled recklessly.

As for Sarazy-Pal, the captives had held him down while two expert torturers had put out his eyes, cut out his tongue and severed his ears, while a delicate artist removed long strips of skin, making the torture last with feline refinements.

A horrible, inextinguishable plaint filled the vast room, and the bodies thrown from the height of the terrace into the sand bounced and then lay still, tragically, at the hazard of the fall.

The surviving women, guided by Starzo, Himroud and Ahmosis, had reached open country beneath the flight of Myrr, the favorite hawk, who was also fleeing the accursed palace in order to rediscover, in a more peaceful retreat, the soft kisses of his dear mistress.

PART TWO

I

IT was the festival of the goddess Mylitta, the Lady of Love and Sensual Pleasure. The temple was illuminated from top to bottom, ornamented with pennants and garlands of foliage.

Inside, Mylitta, crowned with roses, was displayed on a golden throne. Her hair descended in curly ringlets over her shoulders; she was holding a bow and a quiver, the emblems of amour.

All the women of Babylon brought her jewels, with the consequence that the pedestal was covered with them, and near the altar one literally walked upon precious stones.

The priestesses of the goddess remained at prayer for long hours, prostrate before the adorable image, while the dancers executed their most expressive steps and the high-pitched voices of virgins repeated the strophes of the voluptuous hymn indefinitely.

The priestesses were charged particularly with honoring the idol. They supervised its maintenance, sacrificed doves and ewes to the goddess, and renewed the perfumes and flowers that she loved.

The singers and the musicians, sacred courtesans, delivered themselves to the inhabitants of Babylon and rich foreigners who made an adequate offering to the goddess. They sometimes granted a further hour, or a night, to a man who renewed his presents, showing true generosity.

It was on the terraces of the temple, several times a year, that the equally-remunerative sale of virgins was held, for a good part of the money they brought served for the maintenance of the sanctuary. It was further prescribed to every wife to deliver herself to prostitution at least once in her life, in exchange for an honest sum destined for the adornment of "the lady of delights."

Thus, Mylitta was more scintillating than a starry sky, and her temples remained the richest in Babylon. From the city of Cutha to the north to the city of Borsippa in the south, and all the surrounding areas, the gallant arrived in order to present their gifts and claim the amorous suffrage. In Assyria and Chaldea there was no idol more magnificent or more venerated than the lady of the honeyed kisses.

The little priestesses of amour had to abandon all their adornments to the goddess; they circulated freely in the city but any attempt at flight was punished by death. When they pronounced their vows to Mylitta, they could not take them back, and remained in the temple until death. Those who had failed in their duty or withheld some item of jewelry were condemned to the torture of the cross. They were flogged in public and then, after having been exposed on the terrace, they were crucified in the depths of the garden in a special avenue. The vultures soon tore the cadavers apart, and nothing any longer remained on the wood of torture than white skeletons.

Those who remained faithful to Mylitta had a fortunate old age, but their faces, attained by the scourges of time, were covered by dark veils until their final hour. They were employed in the maintenance of the sanctuary; they prepared the incense, renewed the flowers and adorned their companions still in the full bloom of their ephemeral splendor.

The women of the temple displayed pale, slightly unhealthy complexions, and features of a tender and luminous delicacy. Their somber eyes were dying under long eyelids; they trailed silky veils through puddles of perfume, their necklaces and amulets clinking, the flesh and metal priestesses of a magnificent idol.

An odor of incense and aromatics, tenacious and numbing, floated in the air around the columns of onyx, porphyry and marble supporting the vaults of seventeen naves corresponding with seventeen doors. As one advanced into the magical dwelling, the décor seemed to change, rotating with the dancers in an ever-faster rhythm. That was because the intoxication of all the perfumes afflicted the most solid brains, and because all the fervent worshipers of Mylitta were possessed, after a very little time, by the delectable evil of lust.

The door of Nabuchodonosor, which opened in the depths of the temple, was made of a gold plaque encrusted with precious gems; two immense bulls guarded the entrance. The walls of the sanctuary, covered with admirably colored enamels, reflected the light that penetrated there freely, varnishing with fire the immense palace of gold and precious stones, where all the designs and colorations of Chaldean ceramics lit up beneath the flamboyance of the heavens.

The ecstasy of the worshipers of Mylitta, the lascivious lady, comprised seven steps, by which one reached complete felicity.

The first of those steps was the desire of amour, the confused emotion of the senses, within a vague fear of what was about to follow. One saw a thousand gleams therein, with opaline and changing nuances. They floated like flies with indolent, indecisive wings.

The second step was the approach of the kiss. One discovered therein five thousand bright and limpid sapphire blue flames.

The third step was the preliminary caress, the meager delicacies of a curious but still fearful soul. One perceived therein ten thousand gleams the color of ruby, dancing and fantastic, like fire follets. Everything became delectably blurred and took on a beautiful crimson sunset tint. Ardent desire gradually replaced dread; a divine melody lulled the dream of neophytes.

In the fourth step, one saw twenty thousand gleams, inherent to the adorable embrace; they were the color of hyacinth and topaz, emitting a great warmth and causing unfamiliar frissons to pass over the entire body.

The fifth step was that of partial voluptuousness. One experienced, by turns, exquisite, delicate, nuanced sensations like a poem of precious and rare subtlety. Thirty thousand emerald green gleams passed before recklessly blinking dazzled eyes.

The sixth step was that of demi-voluptuousness in the invincible expectation of the great all. One saw therein forty thousand fireflies of all colors, a veritable rain of magically fulgurant precious stones. Nothing any longer remained of terrestrial preoccupations; one floated in the sky in the midst of an angelic concert of infinite softness. A delectable rapture of the mind and body inundated the initiate of celestial intoxications, who understood the goddess in all the mystery of her divine nature.

The seventh step was the perfect intoxication, the summit of human enjoyment, complete, unique, immense, frightful and sublime bliss. There one possessed Mylitta in person, in a stream of fifty thousand suns of a diamantine whiteness. Having reached that state, a man could die, having nothing more to wish for down here.[1]

The singers and dancers of the temple offered themselves to inexperienced neophytes in order to initiate them in the seven steps of perfect sensual pleasure. The lessons were given in special cubicles garnished with silky fabrics, like the alveolae of a beehive. Each cubicle contained an ecstatic couple, and the goddess, from the height of her golden pedestal, presided over the various ceremonies of the cult of amour.

"Glory, glory to Mylitta!" intoned the choir of the faithful, while Menonia, the star dancer, executed her lascivious poses solo, her loins circled by a thin girdle with pendants of precious stones, which did not veil any of her charms; with brilliant plaques trembling over

1 This supposed quotation is untraceable, but might well be authentic; these seven steps of carnal amour echo various accounts of seven steps of divine love found in mystical literature.

her cheeks, she writhed in a slow voluptuousness and indolent grace, scrupulously miming the erotic encounter. Then, agitating flowery branches, clicking bronze castanets shaped like lions' heads, she emphasized her audacious contortions, spinning in an increasingly urgent flight, until the moment when, quivering and unkempt, bathed in sweat, she came to fall at the foot of the altar with a great cry.

II

BUT the bizarre orchestra, composed of triangular harps, double reed flutes and lyres with five strings, suddenly stopped. A loud noise had burst forth at one of the doors of the temple, which the faithful were defending jealously.

A woman with scattered hair and haggard eyes, cleaving through the crowd, advanced all the way to the statue of Mylitta.

"Goddess of love and glory," she said, "have pity on us. We request sanctuary, we put ourselves under your safeguard."

Zazai, the High Priestess, made a sign and all tumult ceased.

"Who are you?" she asked the newcomer, who was embracing her knees.

"I am Himroud, the wife of the satrap Ahassuru."

"Why have you quit his dwelling?"

"Because he wanted my death. I have fled with a few slaves and Ahmosis, whom the satrap wanted to put in my place."

"Let those women enter," said Zazai, authoritatively. "They are under the protection of the goddess."

Ahmosis and her companions came, all trembling, to huddle near the altar, while a great tumult burst forth again outside.

"That's Ahassuru, coming to reclaim his property," groaned Himroud. "We fled his soldiers, and we're so exhausted that we couldn't go any further. All our hope is therefore in you, divine priestess of Mylitta."

"The satrap shall not enter," said Zazai. "The temple of the goddess is sacred; no one can penetrate here without my authorization. Close the doors."

Immediately, the seven golden doors were closed, and the sanctuary became a safe refuge, a prison scintillating with precious stones, which no human power, even that of the king, could violate.

Ahmosis and Himroud were prostrate in a profound adoration. They were praying with all the fervor of their souls, all the ardor of their desire and gratitude.

The songs had resumed with greater force. The harps, mandoras and lyres resonated under the agile fingers that plucked the sonorous strings with gentle vibrations. Before the prostrate fugitives the dances recommenced, for nothing was allowed to interrupt the homage rendered to Mylitta.

Long wisps of hair flagellated the cheeks of pretty girls incessantly in motion. Their torsos undulated with enlacing and serpentine grace; the pendants of their girdles rattled over their rounded loins and over their round thighs, wiry and strong.

After the impetuosity of the first figures they resumed their lascivious, softly caressant poses; their large eyes shone between the antimony lines of their eyelids, and their fine teeth scintillated behind the crimson line of their florid lips, avid for kisses.

After the dances and the songs, wines the color of blood and the sun were circulated. Menonia, the star dancer, drew the liqueur of forgetfulness and ecstasy from two large golden vases ornamented with symbolic figures. Her long-stemmed metal ladle then filled the cups that the assistants held. Frail virgins with flowered gazes passed by with baskets full of jasmine petals, and the perfumed flowers were mingled with the divine beverage.

Soon the faithful, fainting with amour and desire, threw themselves upon the priestesses, and dancers and the singers of the goddess. They were swooning with joy, while the rumor of an entire people in delirium burst forth more formidably outside. It was a rumble of thunder, the protestation of the crowd excluded from the delectable feast by virtue of the satrap's intervention.

Ahassuru, threatened with death in spite of the respect habitually accorded to the chiefs, had drawn away with his soldiers, and the High Priestess, reassured, had the doors of the temple opened again, in order that the voluptuous transports of the disciples of Mylitta would not be lost for the crowd.

III

"YOU'VE done well to come, Ahmosis; I was expecting you."

Menonia, the star dancer, caressed the girl that she had seen for the first time at the temple auction sale.

In order to be recognized by her protectress, Ahmosis had put on her roseate coral hood, the pale pearls of which quivered over her cheeks. She had left all her other jewels in the satrap's dwelling, for she did not want to conserve any gift of the accursed husband. She had found shelter in the temple of Mylitta and she hoped to merit the favor of the goddess.

"Yes," she said, "I've come because you addressed affectionate words to me, and I sensed that I could have confidence in you.

"The satrap wanted to kill you, as he has killed his other wives?"

"You know him, then?"

"We all know him here, for he never misses the temple sales, but the unfortunates he takes away never reappear. Their bones are scattered in the ditches, in company with those of tortured prisoners. I knew by

100

virtue of an oracle of the goddess that you would escape the common fate and that you would return to us with Himroud, the penultimate wife of the tyrant."

"Yes, Starzo saved us."

"Starzo, your lover?"

"No, Starzo my friend and protector."

"Why isn't he with you?"

"Oh," said Ahmosis weeping, "I don't know what has become of him, and I'm dying of anguish. As we were approaching Babylon he disappeared suddenly, and no one has been able to give me news of him."

"We'll find him again."

"May you speak the truth, Menonia! However, if he's been captured by the satrap's soldiers, it's all over for him."

"You know, little Ahmosis, that it is given to the priestesses of Mylitta to penetrate the future. Although, as yet, I'm only an adroit and privileged dancer, I'm rarely mistaken in my presentiments. Your beloved Starzo will be returned to you."

Forgetting her tears, Ahmosis embraced her new friend.

"It's him who prepared our flight. Without his intervention we'd still be in the satrap's horrible dwelling, at the mercy of the guards and eunuchs. Oh, we've suffered a great deal along the road, for it was necessary to hide continually in the reeds of the bank."

The young woman shivered at that fearful evocation. She had drawn Menonia into the garden of the temple, where the moon was shining faintly. Everything was silent now in the voluptuous refuge, after the intoxications and mad embraces of the day. The musicians and the dancers had fallen asleep under the flight of the last kisses, which were doubtless still palpitating in their dreams like beautiful butterflies of flame. Mylitta, upright on her golden throne, opened her eyes enigmatically, sure of her power, for she alone reigned eternally over the earth.

"Oh, how joyful my heart is," murmured Ahmosis, whose youth rendered her serene and confident. "When my beloved has returned to me, I shall have nothing more to desire down here."

She smiled in the gentle light, and her visage took on a strange tint; one might have thought her a golden statue reflecting the moonlight. An adorable mystery enveloped her svelte body, made of mysticism and carnal attraction.

"He's handsome, my Starzo," she said. "Don't you know him?"

"Perhaps I've seen him on the banks of the Euphrates," Menonia murmured, with a sudden and singular melancholy.

"You might have seen him, and spoken to him?"

"No, I wouldn't have had anything to say to him; our destinies are so different."

"That's true; you wouldn't be able to think about a simple boatman. He couldn't pay for a priestess of Mylitta, and the rules are formal."

"Oh," said the dancer, "you love him, and that's sufficient for my desires not to settle on him. In any case, I've never distinguished any man. All those who have possessed me have satisfied my senses without awakening anything in my soul other than curiosity. I put all my fantasies into my vivid and passionate dancing. I mime free, ardent, ineffable amour. I give myself the bliss of the dream that I pursue with my random lovers, but they are nothing in my heart."

Under the moonlight, she snorted like an incensed mare, arching her back, extending her arms toward her fictitious good fortune.

Ahmosis stretched herself limply, recovered from her alarm. She too summoned desire by means of voluptuous poses, palpitating smiles fleeing from her fresh lips only to reappear a moment later.

"Do you know," said Menonia, "that you would make one of the prettiest priestesses of the temple of amour?"

"Me? But I haven't learned anything."

"I'll give you lessons."

"What, you'd consent . . . ?"

"Certainly, to ensure your sojourn here. Otherwise, you'll be sent away after a few days."

"What about Himroud?"

"Himroud, similarly, can only stay on condition of becoming a priestess."

"She could sing for the goddess and pay the harp in the temple. Her voice is marvelous and her playing quite expert."

"I'll speak for her, as for you."

"Oh, how good you are, and how I love you!"

"Do you love me as much as your handsome boatman?" asked the dancer, smiling.

"I love you differently, but my heart can contain several tendernesses."

"Just like mine," said Menonia gravely. "I love Mylitta, the gods, my homeland and my little companion."

The breeze was scented by musk and incense. It rolled in gusts as soft as caresses. For the two friends, the very notion of time was effaced. Sitting in the lunar light, they hugged one another gently, entirely given to amour next to that temple of amour. Like languid autumn roses they quickly showed the golden grains of their hearts for the voluptuous joy of their ephemeral youth. The garden of Mylitta had the funerary repose of a cemetery, the silence of the enclosure of souls, an ardent, melancholy greenhouse full of regrets and intoxication. Immense moths were fluttering heavily over swooning plants.

In the distance, the Euphrates cast a fringe of foam over its banks. The blue edifices, bathed in an immaterial mist, rose up into the sky, breaking it up with their summits, extended like swords. Nocturnal birds brushed them with lowered wings, and Ahmosis was surprised to be alive, to know other possessions than that of the evil and brutal male who had violated her. She was no longer plaintive as well as unsatisfied, discouraged in her youth and her aspirations. Everything acted upon her impressionable and vibrant senses, everything penetrated her with an adorable languor.

"Remain thus, Menonia, your arms on my shoulders, your cheek next to mine. I love the friction of your flesh, the pure perfume of your breath, which reminds me of a rose-bush. I love your large metallic eyes and your firm breasts. Your entire being is entering into me delectably."

"Oh, little Ahmosis, you don't know the slow intoxication of the caress. Your hands have never quivered at the contact of a fresh and supple dermis; your lips have never known the tender kisses of a female mouth. But everything around us is inciting us to the felicity of the embrace. The air is replete with moist perfumes that rise like an intoxicating vapor; it's a divine sound of melodious whispers, of swooning birdsong. Sighs are born from the waters, the quays, the mysterious terraces; it's the exquisite hour when enlaced couples surrender to the joy of loving."

"Yes, I love, I want to love! Is there any other happiness down here?"

"Alas, no! Everything is only pretence and dupery, except for the kiss. The kiss alone makes life worthwhile. Without it, there is no existence, and no death. To escape its adorable spell, you could consult every oracle, every sorceress, every pythoness . . . but human science would be impotent against the law of amour!"

"And yet, you aren't sensible to the embrace of your lovers in the temple?"

"I love amour, all the same. I love it in thought, in aspiration, in dream. I sense it palpitating over your heart, your mouth, in your eyes. In truth, little Ahmosis, if I've taught you the felicity of the senses, you've informed me of the felicity of the soul."

IV

WHEN daylight appeared, Zazai, the High Priestess of the temple, was surprised not to see Menonia dancing before the goddess, as she always did when she awoke; for the first concern of the women consecrated to Mylitta was to honor her altars.

The pale rays of the sun were commencing to play over the enamels of the walls; already, fresh flowers and perfumes had been deposited at the feet of the goddess; slaves shod in palm-fiber sandals were circulating silently, bringing wine, fruits, silver-embroidered veils, cushions and drapes enhanced by precious stones, recent gifts from the ladies of Babylon.

The dancers, Menonia's companions, searched for her under the porticos of the courtyards and on the terraces, thinking that the young woman had perhaps gone to respire the freshness of the dawn along the interior walkways.

Elodoum, a pretty priestess with a pale bronze body, glaucous eyes and a fleshy mouth, came back laughing.

"Menonia," she said, "is asleep in the arms of the satrap's wife! They're lying in the garden next to the fountain."

"Yes," supported Maines, the most cunning of the temple dancers, "they're still smiling at their dream. Truly, it's a very beautiful sight!"

Everyone ran into the garden to see the two friends asleep among the flowers. Their slumber was so profound that the bursts of laughter and whispers were unable to extract them from their torpor.

But Zazai, the High Priestess, frowned, for she desired the daughters of Mylitta to be, above all, at the disposal of the rich amateurs of the city, and these games rendered them indifferent to other caresses.

Ahmosis, however, woke up, and her surprised gaze wandered over the faces leaning over hers.

"Oh!" she said, getting up in confusion. "Doubtless I've merited a terrible chastisement. Dispose of me; I'm ready to submit to any punishment for the sin that I've committed."

Zazai reassured her, while she readjusted her veils and replaced her pink coral hood, which had slipped over her ear, over her forehead.

"Menonia alone has incurred the wrath of the goddess. She ought not to have initiated you into the secrets of amour."

The dancer, sobered, lowered her eyes. "Indeed," she said, "I've forgotten my duties. But Ahmosis was so troubled that I wanted to console her."

"The satrap's wife must quit this dwelling today, since she has been unable to recognize the benefits of Mylitta worthily."

"Mercy!" moaned Ahmosis, falling to her knees. "Don't expel me!"

107

"It's necessary," said Zazai, severely. "We don't have the right to retain for more than a few days women who don't belong to the temple or who come, at least once in their life, to prostitute themselves, obedient to the laws of Babylon."

Ahmosis turned to Menonia, who had promised to defend her, pleading.

The little dancer prostrated herself before the priestess and kissed her knees devotedly.

"It isn't permitted to conserve in the sanctuary women who are foreign to the cult, but we always need dancers and singers. I'll teach my art to the satrap's wife. She's very young, slim and supple; she'll learn the most expert steps quickly, and will be one attraction more for the faithful of Mylitta."

Zazai reflected. "Truly? What can she do?"

"She already knows how to sing and play the harp, as her companion Himroud does. She's not unaware of the ordinary dances of the nomadic tribes, because old Morphy made her beg along the roads. She's even skillful in that primitive art. With a few lessons, she'll be almost as knowledgeable as me."

"She's a pretty girl," said Zazai, who circled the child, examining her like a connoisseur.

"We can never have too many well-turned and adroit women."

"That's true; the temples of Nirgal and Bit-Zida have taken possession of the best subjects, although Mylitta ought to have every preference."

"It's because amour is declining in Babylon. The people prefer the frightful tortures on the banks of the

Euphrates to the sight of gallant pleasures. People no longer live to love, but to destroy one another."

"Ah," said Elodium, the young woman with the glaucous eyes, "we're often idle; it only at the great festivals nowadays that the crowds cluster at the doors of the temple."

"In ten days," sighed Maines, "I've only been summoned to the chamber of amour twice."

"In that time," said Tagyr, a lyre-player with supple arms, "I've only played once the hymn of perfect voluptuousness, which pleases the young people of the city."

Ararhu, a serpentine dancer, made a gesture of discouragement. "I no longer mime the steps of slow passion, except for the priests of Cutha who come here to distract themselves from the severity of their priesthood."

"Doubtless," said Zazai, half-convinced, "new elements of grace and youth might render the temple its former splendor; but it's necessary that neophytes are subjected to serious proofs and to pronounce vows. I'd like nothing better than to welcome the satrap's two wives, if they truly have the firm intention of consecrating themselves to Mylitta."

As Ahmosis hesitated to respond, Menonia pinched her arm gently.

"Always say yes," she whispered, "it's salvation."

"I will consecrate myself to the goddess," Ahmosis said, in a firm voice.

"And your companion Himroud?"

"I don't know her decision."

"Someone go and find her," said the High Priestess, "and tell her that we're waiting for her."

Two dancers drew away at a run, and came back after a brief interval with the young woman.

The latter was very dejected, for she knew that she could only remain in the temple for a few days. Ahassuru would certainly be able to find her again, and nothing equaled the cruelties of his hatred. The most somber imaginations had tortured the unfortunate young woman, who had not ceased weeping since the previous day.

Ahmosis embraced her tenderly. "Dry your tears," she said. "We can stay under the protection of the goddess, if you accept her conditions."

"Oh!" said Himroud, delightedly. "I only ask to serve Mylitta; I won't recoil before any sacrifice in order to please her."

"Do you want to consecrate your life to her?"

"With all my heart."

"And you'll pronounce eternal vows?" said Zazai.

"Immediately, if necessary."

"You'll have no other pleasures, no other wishes, except those accorded to you by Our Lady of Sensual Pleasure?"

"I swear it."

"You'll be able to serve her faithfully in every circumstance, support her and defend her?"

"I'll allow myself to be killed for her!"

"That's good," said Zazai, with satisfaction. "I can see that your vocation is serious. Tomorrow, we'll put it to the proof, and if we're satisfied with you, you'll soon be our equal."

Himroud prostrated herself and kissed the long veil of the priestess, who lifted her up benevolently.

At that moment, a large bird of prey swooped over the young woman's head, uttering a shrill cry. The daughters of Mylitta recoiled in terror, putting their tremulous hands over their faces.

"That's a bad omen," said Zazaai.

But the satrap's wife extended her wrist, smiling, and the hawk came to alight there gently, flapping his wings.

"This is Myrr," she said, "my companion in captivity. He's as gentle as a pigeon, and has remained faithful to me through all proofs."

"You've accomplished a miracle," said the priestess, "for no one has yet been able to tame one of those cruel birds."

Myrr pecked the lips of his mistress tenderly, closing his yellow eyes in an ardent bliss.

"Let him stay with you," said Zazai. "We'll consecrate him to the goddess."

Ahmosis promised in her turn to devote herself to the cult of amour, to follow Mylitta humbly, to honor her all times and in all places.

Two doves were immolated at the feet of the idol, in the fumes of incense and aromatics, while the priestesses officiated in great pomp in order to celebrate the entry of two new queens of joy into the temple of sensual pleasure.

V

HIMROUD, having no lover, gave herself entirely to amour, but Ahmosis begged her friend to substitute for her with the rich lords who came to sacrifice to the goddess.

"I don't want to deceive my dear Starrzo," she said. "Be generous, Menonia; what does one offering more or less matter to you, in the habitual sacrifice of your body?"

Menonia yawned, closing her darkly circled eyelids. "I'm so tired, little Ahmosis."

"One more effort. It will be counted for you later in the valley of all bliss."

"One day or another, the substitution will be perceived."

"Who would complain about it? Are you not the prettiest dancer in the temple."

"I can't satisfy all tastes."

"Bah! Kisses are similar in the dark."

And it was thus that Ahmosis, who only gave herself in the dark, was nicknamed the "mystery lady." At the moment of possession she hid behind a curtain, and Menonia swiftly took her place.

In any case, that game was quite piquant for girls of fifteen and seventeen years of age, who already made fun of the weakness and credulity of men.

When no one presented himself in order to demand their assistance, they went out into the country, hidden under long veils, trying to find Starzo.

They advanced rapidly over burning sand after having quit the skiff that bought them from the gates of Babylon. Hidden in the reeds along the bank of the Euphrates they appealed to their handsome boatman in tremulous voices.

"Starzo! My dear Starzo!" said Ahmosis. "Show yourself, I beg you. It's me, it's your little friend!"

Only the echoes responded to her desolate voice.

Soon, they were walking between the files of torture-victims who bordered the river. Cadavers were swaying in the trees, hands and feet already dissected and desiccated, barring their route. Vultures flew over head, shreds of human flesh in their beaks. In the distance, soldiers were dragging prisoners, marching in the glare of the sun, which cut through them and blinded them.

Sometimes, a wounded man remained in the sand, covered with a red cloth. They approached him furtively, examining him with rapid heartbeats, in the dread and the hope of recognizing the person for whom they were searching.

Then, weary, having wandered for hours, they sat down at the water's edge, and the setting sun, which caressed them, seemed to put all the blood of roses into a crimson aureole around them.

"Oh," sighed Ahmosis, "my beloved is dead. Could he neglect like this the person that he cherished with such a profound amour?"

Menonia did not lose confidence however.

"A voice in the depths of my being cries out to me that he's alive and that he will soon return. Let's not be discouraged, little Ahmosis."

Boatmen were asleep here and there. Interrogated, they responded that they had not seen their companion. Only one said that Starzo might well be in the vicinity of the satrap Ahassuru's dwelling, for he had the habit of heading in that direction. But the two women dared not go that far, even though their veils were thick enough to hide them from all gazes.

They returned to the temple, sad and disappointed, sat down on the flagstones in an attitude of great fatigue, and remained silent under the reproaches of the High Priestess, who criticized those unusual excursions, not understanding their purpose.

VI

THE meditations and the aspirations of the pretty dancers were made of the desire for something that would complete them. A passionate and unconscious ardor sustained them and guided them in their research. Both of them aspired to the amour of the heart, that gift of the self, mysteriously intimate and a thousand times more precious than the gift of the body.

Those frail dreamers suffered from a good fortune glimpsed but still inaccessible, which would have transported them into a paradise of delights.

They made their amorous confidences to one another in a grave and warm tone that penetrated their veins sensually, numbing them feverishly. Charming and secret, even so, they filled one another up mutually with sensuality; nothing was more troubling than their veiled gaze, their smile, sometimes so nostalgic, and the quivering ardor of their young lips.

"That's how I would like to possess the man I love!" said Ahmosis, sliding her supple arm under her friend's. "Put your head on my shoulder and murmur those words to me so sweet that they can only emerge from the mouths of lovers. My youth is a tomb in which I have laid nothing of what I regret. My desires have never been granted! I'm only saddened by not having profited from my light years to give myself to my beloved."

"You'll have a long life."

"Who knows?"

"Everything will succeed for you one day; I sense the contentment of it in my heart."

"I only ask the gods for the return of my beloved."

"He'll come back."

"May you be speaking truly! How I would cherish you if you deigned to hasten the course of events."

"That isn't in my power, my lovely flower of Heaven. I'm only a humble servant of Mylitta. It's her to whom it's necessary to pray, with all the fervor of amour."

They plunged then into long ecstasies, extended before the idol. Their bare feet, circled with gold, appealed for the kiss. Their round shoulders were crushed on the flagstones damp with perfume; but nothing existed for them except the adorable presence of the goddess.

Ahmosis and Menonia both possessed the souls of generous and naïve little girls; outside of their amiable work and the cult of Mylitta, they were never bored. While the satrap's wife intoxicated herself with the memory of the handsome boatman, the little star dancer had lighter occupations; she played with the large monkeys of the temple or teased the sacred cats. The latter came to rub against her legs, purring, arching their backs and sticking up their tails. They were tawny, with black feet and muzzles. Nothing equaled their greed or their agility. They wandered under the porticos in bands of ten or twenty, and their fiery eyes shone in the shadows.

Menonia, with her supple body and her brilliant eyes, resembled the mysterious felines, whose claws could sometimes be felt beneath the velvet paws. In her moments of lascivious enervation, she scratched her frail friend gently, and then threw herself into her arms, laughing.

"Strange desires take me," she said, "to try my fingernails on your flesh; I'd like to bite you like Lorq, my favorite tomcat. It's true that he sticks out his pink tongue immediately, in order to efface the trace of his misdeeds. He's cruel and caressant, voluptuous and perfidious, always unexpected. Don't you think that cats have the souls of courtesans?"

She kissed Lorq, who let her do it, his eyelids half-closed, his eyes drowned in amour; and his grateful purr rattled more loudly, his fur had tremors of pleasure under the young woman's expert fingers.

Ahmosis smiled vaguely, her thought absent, her imagination enfevered by delights that she composed with fragments of her dear memories. She had the ashamed expression of a woman who closes her eyes and turns her head in order to hide her tears. The joy of loving entered into her, always and everywhere: via her eyes, which were illuminated by its burning frictions; via her nostrils, which she filled with the odor of incense and aromatics; and via her ears, which listened avidly to the sacred songs of the temple. And she wept with pleasure and with pain, trying in vain to attain her dream.

Menonia's heart, by contrast, remained in the sort of waking slumber in which one feels neither alive nor dead, but in which one hopes for real sensations. Thus far she had been similar to a plant, or a stone in the road, motionless things that drank in the sunlight through every pore. She loved the voluptuous temple, the jewels, the perfumes, the water of the river, the color of sapphire or aquamarine, and the immutably blue sky; but an unknown frisson, subtle and delicious, ran through her veins in the company of the satrap's wife with the amorously swooning soul.

VII

TWO soldiers are quarreling on the terrace of the temple over the possession of Ahmosis. Standing up to one another, they have exchanged hateful gazes and the priestesses have tried in vain to calm them down. There is an odor of crime in the air. Trembling, the little courtesans gather around the combatants.

Two flashes of lightning: the men, maddened by lust and anger, have drawn their daggers. Howling, they have launched themselves at one another; whoever strikes the most accurately and the most often will prevail. The right arm delivers the blows, with an unequaled violence; the left parries skillfully.

The adversaries already have deep wounds, but neither is out of the contest. Blood spurts, splashing the pretty girls, who run away fearfully. There is a pause, and then the battle resumes more furiously, in spite of Zazai's supplications. One of the combatants totters, raises his open hand to his breast, stiffens his muscles, makes superhuman efforts to remain standing. The other, soon struck in his turn, recoils with a horrible plaint. A well-directed thrust has laid bare the bone of the left arm from the elbow to the shoulder. Meanwhile, the blades are red, the ground is red and the men are red, who slip and get up again with the obstinacy particular to their race.

"Mercy!" groans the High Priestess, who sees the gold destined to Mylitta for the sacrifice of amour falling from the combatants' belts.

"Mercy!" cry the little courtesans, who have returned, full of fear and curiosity.

"Mercy!" murmur the singers and the musicians, veiling their faces.

Ahmosis, lost in her dream, does not seem to understand that it is for her that the fête is being given, and that she has the right to be proud of such a passion.

Exhausted, covered in blood, their breasts lacerated, the men are still fighting, hanging on to the branches of bushes in order not to fall. One, more adroit in spite of the red rain that is blinding him, has fallen upon his enemy. His weapon, planted between two ribs, disappears completely into the broth of flesh that it has traversed.

It is over; the victory belongs to him.

With the air of a damned man, he lays out his riches, and those of his companion, at the feet of Ahmosis.

"For one of your smiles," he says.

The satrap's wife finally understands; she makes a gesture of disgust and is about to refuse, but Menonia murmurs in her ear: "He's one of Ahassuru's soldiers; perhaps he'll talk to you about the one you're seeking."

"Oh!" says Ahmosis, fearfully. "That man horrifies me."

"He's almost dying. What have you to fear?"

"To remain alone with him! To receive his caresses!"

"See how he's tottering. He won't demand anything of you; he's weaker than an infant."

"For one of your gazes," repeats the man, extending his mutilated hands toward the young woman.

"So be it," she says gently. "Lean on me."

And slowly, staggering with the wounded man, who weighs upon her shoulder, she leads him to the cubicle of amour, into the padded retreat, garnished with cushions of silken fabric and flowers, where kisses are exchanged.

As usual, Memonia has slipped behind the curtain that masks the couch, ready to intervene at the slightest danger.

"You've come from Ahassuru's camp?" Ahmosis asks the wounded man.

"Indeed, I'm under his orders."

"But how can you have so much money in your possession?"

"It's the product of the booty."

"The war is over, then? You're victorious?"

"Yes."

The man closes his eyes, about to lose consciousness.

"Tell me," says Ahmosis, swiftly. "Do you know what has happened in the satrap's domain?"

"The guards and the eunuchs have been murdered by the prisoners. The slaves have fled; everything has been pillaged."

"And Ahassuru hasn't avenged himself?"

"I don't know," says the soldier, his lips turning blue. "Come closer, give me your mouth so that I can draw life therefrom. Come . . . closer . . . very close . . ."

He is no longer stammering anything but inconsequential words, and falls backwards, uttering a profound sigh.

In spite of her repugnance, the young woman puts her ear to the man's breast. The heart has ceased beating; he is no longer anything but a cadaver.

"Oh, I shan't know anything," she says, sadly, as she emerges from the sinister redoubt.

Menonia puts her arm around her waist, seductively. "The grateful goddess will come to your aid; you've earned such a fine present for her!"

Intoxicated by that savage scene, the little dancer, with feline gestures, inhales the acrid odor emitted by her friend's hair, still impregnated with blood; she lets her lips wander over the short wisps that had brushed the soldier's breast.

Ahmosis is still shivering with terror throughout her body, her breasts feverishly erect like buds after a storm; she presses against her friend's heart, more sensitive to the soft caress. The ordeal that she has just undergone makes the effusion of compassionate pity seem better. Menonia's enigmatic eyes pour their mysterious effluvia toward her; her voice possesses a more penetrating charm . . .

It is an exquisite moment, a divine ray of sunlight after the crime . . .

VIII

THE temple reached toward the sky for the conquest of the stars. The Ziggurat, with the angular
profile, displayed unequal prisms piled one atop another in retreat, crowned with a light edicule where the god
lodged. The stages were as many solid bowls of raw clay,
and the terminal chapel only contained a single chamber ornamented by an altar. Ornaments of blue and
white enameled plaques decorated the exterior walls,
while the precious woods of cedar and cypress paneled
the sanctuary.

Leaves of thin gold laminated parts of the wood-
work, and mosaic panels composed of alabaster, onyx,
cornelian and lapis lazuli alternated with them. The
statue of Mylitta, standing up in stiff and heavy icons
in that discreet location, seemed more tender and more
meditative.

Alongside the terrible gods who persecuted the
Chaldean people, next to those disquieting genii armed
with words and spears, which jutted from the corners
of the walls at every step, the goddess was truly a figure
of peace and grace. Her protective presence drove away

ghouls and fleshless specters which emerged from their tombs to drink the blood of the living.

Those monsters, which were found everywhere else, had the feet of birds and the scales of fish, the tail of a bull and vast outspread wings. Some showed ferocious muzzles and rolled metallic eyes; they had the head of a lion or a vulture, a hyena or a wolf. Others balanced the body of a dog on legs terminated by an eagle's claws. But the most frightful fled under the gaze of the goddess, who only had to lift her little finger in order to be obeyed.

It was to the elevated sanctuary of the Ziggurat that Menonia often dragged her friend. She loved that discreet place, suspended like a nest between heaven and earth. It was there that she studied her new steps, naked before the florid altar, in the vapors of incense and aromatics.

In that fashion, she taught the young woman the dances of Mylitta, which were the most voluptuous in Babylon.

Soon, the pupil was as skillful as her teacher. The goddess had two star dancers, whose lascivious poses attracted numerous adherents. Every evening, at the hour of invocations and sacrifices, it was necessary to open the seventeen golden doors in order to permit the curious to take their places in the temple.

Himroud, who had quickly became habituated to her new mission, had also conquered a certain celebrity by means of the magnificent amplitude of her voice. She put into her resonant song all of human distress, and the burning instinct to live in order to love, the sole joy of existence. She enjoyed liberty now, in the fashion of a beautiful, noble and proud animal; she intoxicated herself with all the drunkenness of intercourse, having nothing to safeguard in her present or in her future. She loved the cool and perfumed temple, the silky cubicle where she gave herself to the feast of amour, the glaucous waters that she could see from the end of the terrace, the long grass of the garden in which she rolled around like a frisky mare, the sky riddled with stars . . .

She sensed all instincts quivering within her, all desires for the beings who passed by, and her beautiful body, a living altar of sensual pleasure, accepted all offerings.

Myrr, the familiar bird, sometimes seemed jealous of the caresses that his dear mistress accorded to others. His fiery eye had a disquieting gleam then; he flapped his wings grimly, launching his savage cry.

The little priestesses were amused by the anger of the handsome bird, which they teased maliciously, knowing full well that, fundamentally, he was gentler than one of the temple pigeons.

"He's almost as affectionate and seductive as the faithful of Mylitta," said Elodoum, the courtesan with the glaucous eyes.

Ararhu, the serpentine dancer, offered her breasts to the great tawny bird, which pecked them gently.

Tagyr, the lyre-player with the supple arms, played him the most tender melodies, like a lover of choice.

But Myrr quit all his little friends in order to follow Himroud, the only one he truly cherished, and nothing could retain him when the young woman had quit the shady gardens.

125

IX

THAT day, they had prayed to the goddess more devoutly, for there was a matter of dancing in the king's palace before the execution of prisoners. On the return from every glorious campaign, a great popular fête was given, which the priestesses of Mylitta honored with their presence.

The crowds had gathered in the hanging gardens and on the terraces in order to admire the king of kings, seated on his golden throne, and his superb militia. Musicians blew into brass horns and long bronze trumpets that made deafening sounds.

The chiefs marched in a radiance of helmets, pikes, javelins and round or rectangular bucklers, their bodies clasped in leather coats with imbrications of iron, in tortoiseshell or wooden armor. Behind them pranced the cavalry, Persians, Medes, Caduceans and Saces, and the satraps of the various provinces.

The priestesses arrived, as was customary, ornamented by their most splendid jewels, crowned with flowers, and more beautiful than all the virgins of Babylonia. They carried Mylitta, the Lady of Amour, whose golden statue loomed up prestigiously in the bright light. They knelt down before Nabuchodonosor's throne, while their musicians played a hymn of war of which the singer intoned the glorious song and the dancers executed their boldest steps.

The king of kings gazed at the priestesses of sensual pleasure with complaisance, for he knew the power of the goddess. He had tinted eyelids and an aquiline nose, and his beard, curled into ringlets and symmetrical braids, hid his thick lips.

The satiation of enjoyment, the disgust of triumphs and the ennui of everything had immobilized his regular features. The most barbaric tortures had difficulty extracting hum from his torpor; he no longer took the trouble to put out the eyes of captured chiefs personally; his senses no longer had any but rare desires.

Nabuchodonosor was coiffed with a gold miter studded with precious stones; a broad gorgerin with nine rows of enamels and gems covered his chest, and his long crimson mantle enveloped him like a veil of blood. Everything about him had a majestic and redoubtable splendor.

The little dancers of Mylitta continued to twirl in the reserved space between the throne and the prisoners of war, chained in pairs.

Behind the latter, chariots with bronze-rimmed wheels were lined up, and cavaliers with gleaming helmets and scaly corselets; above every head the bronze blades of swords, lances, slings and axes were flamboyant.

To the right and the left slaves guarded the booty, and carts filled with bloody trophies. From time to time, the hurricane of the military bands drowned out the sounds of the lyres and flutes. The clarions, drums, sistra and tambourines raged in the immense space, and the priestesses of Mylitta drew breath.

Now it was the turn of Ahmosis and Menonia, the two star dancers. They advanced, confused, with slow steps, rattling the pearls of their necklaces and the rings on their arms. As they went to prostrate themselves before the king of kings, a cry of fury departed from the group of chiefs. Ahassuru had recognized his young wife, and was menacing her with his fist, quivering with impotent rage.

Ahmosis, who knew that she was protected by the goddess, took pleasure from braving the satrap; supple, lascivious, delectable with youth and grace, she was enveloped loosely in a silver veil lighter than a moonbeam. The transparent fabric molded her from head to foot. Then, pirouetting with a vertiginous speed, she emerged from the brilliant sheath, and, naked, exquisite and impeccable, she stopped in front of the royal throne.

A laudatory murmur greeted her savant poses; she was found to be even prettier than in the temple, more desirable in the bright sunlight that made the most of each of her perfections. Menonia associated herself with her prestige, lively, slender and serpentine; her glaucous eyes shone between the painted lines of her eyelids; her ardent lips smile voluptuously. She mimed the poem of amour with a troubling precision, pursuing Ahmosis, who always slipped away, expressing her passion to her in irresistible poses.

Large gold circles beat her cheeks; she twisted, arched her body, knelt down, seemingly imploring the fugitive. Finally, on the tips of her feet, there was a mad race. The dancers grew, took to the air, fluttering like dragonflies. Then Menonia, taking possession of the scarf with lunar reflections, threw herself on to her companion's shoulders as she took her prisoner. Then both of them, enlaced and quivering, came to fall at the monarch's feet.

A frenetic acclamation saluted their triumph. Very emotional, they got to their feet and disappeared into the battalion of the priestesses of Mylitta. Ahmosis, lowering her eyes, seemed to want to hide from the admiring gazes, but an abrupt movement on the part of her companion caused her to raise her head. Then she saw, in the first rank of the prisoners, in chains, covered with blood, Starzo, who seemed to be hardly able to stand up.

"Starzo!" she murmured, in a hoarse voice

"Who? That captive who's devouring you with his eyes?"

"It's him that I love. It's him who saved me."

"But I know him . . ."

"Oh, Menonia, he's doomed! He's going to die!"

They were in midst of their companions, behind the statue of the goddess, and the young woman could deliver herself freely to her despair.

A flame had passed through Menonia's eyes.

"Starzo," she said. "That's Starzo?"

She remembered that the boatman had hidden in the temple one day, after the sale of the virgins, and that she had admired him in the shadows, desiring vaguely to belong to him. His nose with the delicate ridge, his long tender eyes and the perfect oval of his face had made a certain impression on the little dancer and courtesan of Mylitta. She no longer found, in the expressive head of the young man, the coppery red complexion, thick beard and harsh eyes of the Babylonians. His complexion had an olive-tinted pallor, his silkier hair undulated gracefully, his lips, not hidden by a thick fleece, had a tender and charming design.

All that strangeness had moved the previously insensible heart of Menonia. She had often thought about the handsome stranger, without admitting it to herself, but with a significant persistence.

X

THE fête continued in a riot of colors, sounds, dances and drunkenness. Ahmosis, leaning on her friend's shoulder, felt so unhappy, so incapable of living thus, that she would have liked to pick up a weapon in order to pierce her breast. It was flame that was circulating in her veins, setting fire to her mind, ready for the most insensate ventures.

"He's doomed," she repeated, despairingly.

Almost as emotional as the satrap's wife, Menonia remained silent. Swiftly, however, she removed the cluster of roses that retained her hair, and threw it at the prisoner's feet.

Starzo smiled, but his bound hands could not pick up the amorous offering. Only his heart was embalmed by it.

The High Priest, clad in white and mitered in gold, headed toward the august platform, followed by fifty individuals belonging to the sacred order. They were holding sacrificial knives and their hands were red with blood. After having killed innocent ewes for the gods, they were now going to preside over the massacre of men for the worldly powers.

After amour the crowd, habituated to spectacles of complicated and terrible tortures, was clamoring for death. The Syrian, Tyrian and Arabian dancers who had succeeded the courtesans of Mylitta had not had any success. They had retired, confused, tinkling the little bells of their adornments and the medallions in their hair. The Idumeneans and Syrians had designed their most lascivious steps in vain; the people were no longer interested in gracious games and tender pleasures; they required the orgy of quivering flesh, the anguish of slow tortures, without respite and without pity.

The priests lit the sacrificial fires, for it was customary to offer to the gods all the crimes of kings. Slaves stimulated balls of perfume that gave off a thicker smoke, and the singers intoned, to a lugubrious and monotonous rhythm, a hymn to the dead.

Fainting, Ahmosis leaned on the Menonia's shoulder; the latter's eyes were gleaming strangely.

"Can't you do anything to save him?"

"I'm only a little dancer, without influence and without support. What could I attempt, alas, in favor of your beloved?"

"I don't know . . ."

"If the king found you pretty, he might perhaps make the sacrifice of that prisoner in exchange for your kiss."

"The king hasn't even looked at me."

"How do you know?"

"His eyes were wandering at hazard, without fixing on anything. He has the prettiest young women in the world in his harem. What am I compared with them?"

"The new fruit that a blasé monarch might desire for a day."

"Oh, Menonia, if the king of kings would only make a sign! Could not Zazai, the High Priestess, speak for me?"

"Zazau is praying for those about to die."

"She's good, she might have pity."

Ahmosis and Menonia, shoving their companions in order to fray a passage through their tightly packed ranks, have arrived next to the High Priestess, who, only showing the whites of her eyes, with her arms extended, is imploring the goddess.

Mylitta, the Lady of Sensual Pleasure, the Babylonian Venus, is presiding over tortures, while the choir of women recounts her descent into the abode of the dead in the bowels of the earth.

The golden statue dominates the crowd of prisoners in her serene glory, and the executioners are attaching those condemned to noble tortures before the smiling idol. Those first victims will simply have their heads cut off, their rank giving them the right to a relatively clement end. Already, the royal garden is no more than a field of carnage. The perfume of corollas in bloom, the vapors of incense and aromatics are stifled by a sickening and musky odor of butchery, with which the breeze mingled the smoke of the pyres erected to the right and the left.

Blood splashes the foot of the throne and the garments of the sacrificial priests; the gasps of the dying can be heard, and the joyful clamors of the cruel crowd. There is the cracking of dislocated jaws and broken bones, and the hoarse breath of cut throats. Heads separated from the trunk roll, emptying out; limbs dissected with skill are still palpitating.

Nabuchodonosor's nostrils quiver like those of a charger on the battlefield. He inhales the emanations of the warm dead flesh with delight, and a profound sigh swells his breast. He seems to emerge from a dream; his dark eyes have a voluptuous gleam, which Zazai, the High Priests, has seen glide over the courtesans of Mylitta. Now, she knows full well that the odor of blood awakens the dormant desires of the king, who, then disdaining his gynaeceum, sometimes spends a night in the temple.

The sacrificial priests are intoning a kind of chant, the final note of which serves as a signal for each new execution. At the shrill cry of the priests, the executioner's blade falls upon the nape of the neck, severing the head, and the breast of the decapitated man is seen to rise up again under the tumultuous movements of the heart, which continues to beat.

But the knives are becoming blunt and the executioners, fatigued, saw through the necks of the victims, biting into the jaw, the nape or the ear, plunging into the wound several times before succeeding in their hideous task.

Ahmosis has dragged herself to the feet of the High Priestess.

"Mercy!" she says. "Mercy for the man I love!"

The High Priestess interrupts her invocations to the gods of murder and lust.

"Who do you love, then?"

"A prisoner who is about to die."

"And what can I do for him?"

"Ask the king for his life."

"The king wouldn't listen to me, for his thought is absent. And then, what could I offer him in exchange?"

"Me!" says Ahmosis, raising her supplicant hands toward Zazai.

But the High Priestess smiles sadly. "The desires of our master are becoming increasingly rare. He's blasé with regard to the courtesans of Mylitta."

"His gaze, however, was directed toward me. I saw his somber eyes gleaming."

"It was doubtless the pleasure of the murder."

"Or the desire for amour. Is he not more tender on the evening of these massacres?"

"Yes, once he honored the temple with his presence after having seen prisoners of war sacrificed. But a mage made him terrible predictions, and since then, he has disdained the joys of Mylitta. See, his face is not even animated by the most frightful tortures. His visage is like water that no ripple furrows; he remains as impenetrable as death."

Zazai fell silent, not daring to interrupt the king's reverie.

Other captives, their hands bound behind their backs, were led to the torture. These were to perish by strangulation. The executioners wound a cord around their neck, and tightened it by means of a peg, which they rotated in the same direction, very slowly.

A few victims were subjected to more frightful tortures, and their moans were incessant. Long strips of flesh were detached from their bodies, forming complicated arabesques. Then, weary of the game, the sacrificers excised the nipples, the biceps, and the calves. The section of the arms and legs required long labor, the joints of the elbows and knees only ceding after difficult efforts. In spite of that frightful dissection, the martyrs were still alive, and they were only finished off by striking them in the heart.

Ahmosis blocked her ears and veiled her eyes. At the idea that her beloved was doubtless about to be subjected to a similar fate, she uttered a heart-rending scream, which covered the plaints of the victims. The king turned his impassive face toward her; a gleam animated his gaze, and he said a few words to the chief of the eunuchs, who descended the steps of the throne.

XI

"THE king of kings has sent me to you."

"May his will be accomplished; may he live forever," murmured Zazai fervently.

"The master has noticed the young woman who mimed the poem of amour. He desires to visit her this evening in the temple."

"Tell him, Mounoph, that all the priestesses of Mylitta are his humble slaves, and that they are infinitely honored by his choice."

The chief eunuch gave Zazai an initial offering for the goddess and returned to take his place behind the monarch, who did not even seem to perceive his return.

"Are you happy?" Menonia murmured in her friend's ear.

"I'll be happy when Starzo is free."

"He will be. A shadow is falling over Babylon; the people are weary of carnage."

The detachment of heads, the cutting up of limbs and the butchery of entrails was, in fact, slowing down. To the right of the throne, severed hands were piling up; to the left grimaced fearful visages, immobilized in a supreme anguish. The monarch seemed to be floating on a river of blood, and his long crimson mantle was trailing in the red tide that bordered it with a darker fringe.

"There won't be any more killing today," Menonia said, then. "The other captives will be crucified, unless they're destined to be impaled. This evening, you can ask for mercy for Starzo."

"Will the king come?"

"Certainly, since he has promised Zazai."

"And will he deign to demand my caresses?"

"It's necessary not to discourage fate, little Ahmosis. The dread of adversity attracts the anger of the gods to humans. Since chance favors you, don't put it in doubt by chimerical terrors. Take advantage of the benefits that are offered to you."

"Oh, Menonia, I'm trembling like a leaf. Will I be able to satisfy the king of kings?"

"Are you not beautiful among the most beautiful?"

"The monarch has the right to be difficult, for his power is formidable, and his desires command the elements."

She looked at the impassive face of the tyrant, his curved nose, and his cruel, bestially beautiful eyes.

But Nabuchodonosor stood up, and his long crimson mantle, heavy with gold and silver embroideries, dripped blood behind him. His tall tiara, ablaze with rubies and topazes, scintillated under the setting sun. It was the signal for the return to the palace and the end of the massacre.

A great sigh of relief swelled the breasts of the survivors, even though their torture was certain.

Ahmosis and Menonia smiled at Starzo, who returned their smile, forgetful of his suffering and the danger. He no longer felt the bonds that were bruising his arms; he no longer saw the executioners, who, drunk on carnage, were slipping in the red puddles while wiping their broad blades. What did death matter to him, since he had rediscovered amour?

With blows of the lash, the prisoners were driven in front of the war-chariots, and their bonds cut more profoundly into their flesh. Some were secured by the elbows behind the back; some had their necks strangled by a carcan; some were hopping in the short ropes that bound their ankles too closely. An ingenious cruelty had presided over that arrangement, which hampered all their movements, and the guards marching alongside them struck them relentlessly.

Courageously, Starzo remained in his rank, insensible to the ill-treatment, his feet in the mud and his forehead in the azure.

"I love you!" shouted Ahmosis, blowing him a kiss. But her voice was lost in the tumult of bronze-rimmed wheels and the chords of the barbaric music that was celebrating the glory of the conqueror.

The chariots advanced ten by ten, the axles almost touching but never colliding, so skillful were the warriors. The infantry battalions followed in perfect order, making shields, spears and axes glitter. Then came the allied troops with shining helmets, sharpened arrows and heavy slings.

Night fell suddenly, like an immense blue veil thrown over people and things. In that somber azure shone the ingenuous gaze of the stars, astonished to be mirrored in the red river of interminable slaughter and invincible hatred.

XII

"IN order to succeed, it's necessary to put in the urn leaves of mandrake, nightshade and aconite, and vervain flowers."

Menonia pronounces the mysterious words that ought to drive away evil spirits. She desires Starzo's liberty as much as her companion, and she will slip into the monarch's bed at the moment of the embrace, for she is cunning and experienced.

Ahmosis, covered with jewels from head to foot, displays herself more resplendently than Mylitta, whose magical adornment she has borrowed.

"Are you not mistaken?" she asks, anxiously. "Is that really the invocation of the helpful powers?"

"Certainly; I've pronounced it often enough to attract divine favor to me."

"And you've mixed the magic perfumes?"

"I haven't forgotten anything."

"Let the king of kings come, then. I'm in haste to make him the gift of myself, since he can save the Dearly Beloved."

Transfigured, as if by a fateful tide, adorable by virtue of the tenderness that is burning in her eyes and putting a red ember over her childlike mouth, Ahmosis is stirred to the utmost depths of her being.

"Let him come! Let him come!" she sighed, lending an attentive ear to the noises from outside.

And she threw herself into her friend's arms, thinking to embrace her dream. Her desire was bitter and feverish; the minutes had never seemed so long.

"Perhaps he's no longer thinking about me. He must be capricious in his formidable power. Some other woman might have been able to seduce him since his return to the palace. The three queens are beautiful, and the royal gynaeceum contains admirable slaves of amour. I'm dying of impatience!"

"The hour has not yet sounded, little Ahmosis."

Slowly, Menonia caresses her companion's forehead with her lips. She too is wishing ardently for the arrival of the monarch, for she is secretly in love with the handsome boatman and will spare nothing to obtain his liberation. Ahmosis does not know the kisses that drain the greatest energies and deliver a submissive man to the whim of his lover; she has not learned the rare sensualities that plunge a man into the intoxication of the dream and leave him, on awakening, weaker than an infant. Menonia, the courtesan of the temple and the pupil of the gods of lust, will be able to vanquish the royal will. No one can resist the ardent priestesses of Mylitta!

But a hymn of thanks bursts forth in the temple. Nabuchodonosor has come, to seek in the arms of a skillful lover the forgetfulness of power and the bitterness of his reign.

He hopes to calm the dolorous frisson that runs through his being, to forget the distress of living and the fear of death. He regrets that which might have been and has not been; he suffers from his vain cruelties; he has a clear perception of the infinite misery of which even the existence of a king is woven.

Yes, all the sumptuousness of his reign is merely the dreams of a shadow, and after some years of incoherent and weary life, he will have ceased to agitate, in order to return to the great slumber that finally embraces all beings down here. What use are his past glories, the conquest of Egypt and the destruction of the kingdom of Juda? The prophets have predicted that he will lose his reason, and that, metamorphosed into a beast, he will live in savage places, browsing the grass of ravines and slaking his thirst in the turbid water of pools.

A penetrating and unhealthy influence is emitted from the trees, the walls, the plants, from everything he sees and everything he touches; something supreme emerges for him from female eyes with a sad and languorous flame. He senses a poetry of adieu there, a sweetness of agony, a soul of distress and forgiveness.

The cruel tyrant is worn out by murders; the sight of blood horrifies him, and he will certainly grant to the friend of an evening the mercy she desires. If he were free to send back all the prisoners, perhaps he would do it, but the satraps demand the habitual butchery, the people only delight in the sight of slow death-throes and frightful tortures.

XIII

"ROCK me, little flower of the sacred pools. I am weary this evening, weary to the point of death. My eyes are full of a red light that does not want to be extinguished; it is a sinister veil, which even covers your face, falling from the vault of the temple and trailing over the steps of the altar. Do you not also have that frightful flame in the gaze?"

"No, Master of the World, torch of human destinies. I see you as you are, as powerful and as beautiful as the sun."

"Truly, you see me thus, dear Smile of my heart?"

"Yes, I contemplate you in all your serene majesty, I venerate you and I love you."

"Oh, if you could render me confidence and hope, I would grant all your desires."

"I will pray to Mylitta, who disposes of human destinies."

"Will she be able to relieve me of the sinister prediction of the priests of Israel?"

"Certainly, for she has all the powers. Amour will always be the master down here. There is only amour and death. All the rest is lies."

"However, my nights are poisoned by sinister visions. I no longer have a single minute of repose or joy; my will flexes before a formidable and mysterious power."

"When you have savored my kisses, when I will have surrounded you with an intoxicating atmosphere, you will forget all your chimerical fears. The evil predictions will evaporate like incense over embers Do you not have Babylon and Nineveh, those two incomparable jewels? Are you not the master of the most powerful nations? You have conquered more glory than all the monarchs who have preceded you. If the world is insufficient for you, you could extend your ambition to the stars and dethrone the gods. Don't listen to the blasphemies of tenebrous spirits who are jealous of your power. Raise your forehead toward the stars, O King of Kings, Lord of all that exists, Son of the Gods and the Sun!"

Ahmosis was prostrate before the august visitor, who deigned to listen to her with benevolence. She was prey to a singular disturbance that precipitated the beating of her heart. Although she was sensible to the honor of having inspired a rare desire in the conqueror, in the solemn, frightening and superb being who was fixing his troubled gaze upon her, she did not experience any real sympathy for him. Only the ardent determination to liberate her friend was driving her to this submission. To the blasé and sanguinary king who desired her carnal caresses, she could not give her soul.

However, she pressed herself against him, uncovering her young and charming body, which, thanks to the complicity of Menonia, had only been subjected, as yet, to the embraces of the satrap, her husband.

The king had risen to his feet and guided her to the chamber of amour, while the choir of priestesses who were celebrating the immense honor of having stimulated the master of the world sang more loudly.

"What do you want?" asked the royal lover, after the first caresses.

"I dare not speak," she said, shivering. "What I would like is very little to you, but I value it more than existence, and your refusal would kill me."

"Tell me without dread your heart's desire. I will realize it."

Ahmosis kissed the king's knees, not daring to raise her blushing face toward him.

"Speak," he said, again.

"Oh," she sighed, "I only ask you for the life of a captive."

"The life of a captive?"

"Yes," she said, faintly.

"Is he your husband, your brother or your lover?"

"He's my friend, the person who protected my childhood and always watched over me."

"He's a powerful chief, then?"

"No, he's a boatman."

"A boatman! You, a priestess of Mylitta!"

"My friend is handsome and brave. He would be worthy to serve the gods."

"Truly?" said the king. "And what is his name?"

"His name is Starzo. He's a foreigner, like me."

"He's a prisoner of war, then?"

"He hasn't fought against you, since he remained in Babylon."

"He's betrayed his country, then?"

"Oh, no, powerful master! You can't know . . . but I'll tell you everything. I'm the wife of the satrap Ahassuru, who wanted my death. Starzo saved me, and is doubtless expiating that courageous action. Do you understand, now? While I was fleeing, the soldiers captured him in order to torture him, and mingled him with the other captives. I took refuge in the temple of Mylitta, knowing that the sanctuary is inviolable. The goddess protects me henceforth. O King of Kings, lord of the sands, the waves and the forests, save the humble boatman who watched over my days!"

"I will grant your friend mercy," said the king, wearily.

And he gave Ahmosis the imprint of his royal seal, which would open the door of the dungeons to her.

The little dancer prostrated herself again, so joyful and so emotional that she could not find words to express her gratitude.

She arranged fifteen flowery sprigs in baskets around her; she had lips of honey and arms softer than lotus stems. The blasé tyrant wanted to draw her against him in order to slake his thirst for kisses and caresses at length, but a somber veil descended over his reason; he uttered a lugubrious groan and was terrified by the vision of his imminent tortures, and the destruction of Babylon.

XIV

"I'M happy, Menonia, happier than I've ever been!"
Ahmosis was holding, delicately, a little cornelian statue that ought to protect her against all maleficent spells. She headed for the dungeons, fearful and
smiling. Her friend accompanied her, carrying flowers
and perfumes. They were both going to liberate the
prisoner; they were marching rapidly, at the pace of a
scampering bird. Curiously, they interrogated the somber streets, the imposing palaces, the granite monsters,
the squares swarming with people, fearful of being recognized; but thick veils covered their faces, and no one
seemed to notice them amid the comings and goings of
slaves and merchants.

"May the goddess protect us!" sighed Ahmosis,
putting the little cornelian idol, a miniature of Mylitta,
Lady of Sensual Pleasure, to her lips.

"Oh, how my heart is beating!"

"Nothing, henceforth, can separate me from Starzo.
The king is going to send me a hundred gold talents; he
promised me that. My dear lover is waiting for me, for I
wanted to free him myself. Hurry up, Menonia!"

147

"I'm completely out of breath."

"I nearly dropped the goddess."

"Hold her firmly against your breast, for she'll avenge herself cruelly if her dear image is damaged."

The little courtesans had arrived at the door of the prisons. It was an immense city in which thousands of wretches destined for the worst tortures often languished.

Broad and deep moats surrounded the walls. Sentinels marched along their crenellations night and day, in hourly relays, to the formidable sound of a trumpet which howled from rampart to rampart.

The guards only lifted the chains of the entrance on royal orders. Ahmosis presented the wax imprint that Nabuchodonosor had given her. The suspicious colossus who interrogated her immediately stood aside with great respect. The little dancers crossed the redoubtable threshold that the prisoners only crossed in order to go to death. A guide conducted them through low courtyards and obscure channels bordered by cells to the subterranean hall that Starzo occupied, with five hundred captives.

The young man, secretly alerted, was waiting for his friend. When he perceived her, he uttered a great cry of joy, and clasped her to his heart passionately.

"Oh, Starzo!" she moaned.

"Adored darling!"

The prisoners around them had ceased their laments, so much does amour have attractions, even for the most unfortunate.

"King's order!" said the guardian.

There was a long murmur of astonishment, for the condemned of war were never granted mercy.

"You're free!" cried Ahmosis.

"Not yet," said the man, with a coarse snigger. "The royal seal authorizes me to let you visit the captive, but I don't have the right to open the doors of the prison."

"And when will you have that right?" asked the anxious young woman.

"This evening, perhaps tomorrow . . ."

"We'll come back this evening, we'll come back tomorrow . . ."

"We'll come back," said Menonia, enveloping Starzo with a burning gaze.

The handsome boatman shivered under the tones of that vibrant voice. He had stuck into his loincloth the bunch of roses that the courtesan had thrown to him, and which a soldier had been kind enough to pick up for him.

"It's you," he said, "that I saw yesterday on the field of torture? You danced with Ahmosis before the goddess? Both of you were so perfectly beautiful that my eyes didn't quit you for an instant."

"Menonia has helped me in this dolorous ordeal," said Ahmosis. "She's a true friend."

"Oh, I was glad to serve you," replied the little courtesan, swiftly. "You can count on my devotion." She had taken Starzo's hand, and squeezed it tenderly.

"But how do you come to be among the captives?" Ahmosis asked.

"I was protecting your escape, and I was perceived by a soldier whom the treason of a slave had put on your track. All the satrap's prisoners were similarly re-captured, and subject to the same fate. They were too weak to fight against solidly armed warriors; they had scarcely finished massacring the palace guards and the eunuch Sarazy-Pal when the satrap's troops reduced them to impotence. But you were able to get away and take refuge in the temple of Mylittis; my dearest wish was accomplished."

"We'll save you too, my Starzo."

"The goddess will help us."

It required all the ineffable intoxication of amour to permit the two women to remain in that horrible place, which no one ever visited. The dead remained mingled pell-mell with the living there. They decomposed slowly, showing convulsed faces that seemed still to be howling a final blasphemy. Some were laughing atrociously; others, twisted by pain, seemed prey to a superhuman terror. Bones pushed against the walls formed a white mass there, covered with detritus of every sort. What did that frightful vicinity matter to those men who were going to die? Captives never remained for more than a few days in those waiting rooms, and those who perished before the torture were the privileged. Many, in any case, killed themselves, or had their companions strangle them when no weapon could be filched from the guards.

Madmen were singing a warrior hymn on one corner; the dying were convulsing on the floor, into which they were digging their clenched fists. Others, in spite of the frightful heat, were shivering and clicking their teeth. It was a sinister and macabre human herd, which would have made the little courtesans shiver if they had not been sustained by their passionate dream.

"Come on, let's go," moaned Ahmosis, however, less habituated than her companion to the spectacle of human dolors. She had seized Starzo's arm, and was trying to draw him away.

"No one leaves," said the guard, shoving her back brutally. "Have you forgotten?"

"That's true, I'd forgotten. Would you like my jewels, my clasps, my rings, my necklaces?"

The man considered her with disdain. "Where are your riches, then? You're less adorned than a daughter of the people."

The priestesses of Mylitta were not, in fact, wearing any jewelry, for fear of attracting attention.

"You'll be satisfied tomorrow," said Ahmosis, blushing.

Menonia had put her flowers at the prisoner's feet; she spread perfume and balms over him, murmuring vague incantations.

Ahmosis presented the cornelian statuette to her lover's lips. "Kiss the Lady of Sensual Pleasure," she said, "and may your heart be penetrated by amour. She has always rewarded faithful lovers."

But the guardian uttered a guttural appeal; a bronze gong vibrated lugubriously, and the door of the dungeon opened to let the visitors pass.

"Soon, my beloved!"

"Soon," said Menonia, also, smiling at the handsome boatman.

XV

THE two friends could not leave the temple that evening, for there was a sacrifice to the goddess, and all the daughters of Mylitta had to attend the ceremony.

Menonia had prayed with a very particular fervor, giving her friend precious advice.

"We'll succeed," she said, "for the Lady of Amour is with us. I've interrogated her in a whisper, and she has replied to me."

"It's necessary also to beg her not to cease protecting us. I'll give her all the adornments that I owe to the king's caprice. I received a coffer this morning encrusted with agates and hematites, which I haven't even opened. It's very heavy, for two slaves could hardly carry it."

The courtesans went on to the terrace, where the priestesses were already assembled for the habitual sacrifices. The sky was a profound blue, and the Milky Way was shimmering in light wavelets in the ocean of azure. Intoxicating aromas were disengaged by swooning corollas; a continuous breeze came from the hanging gardens, a voluptuous breath that intoxicated the mind and troubled the senses.

Zazai, covered by a long white veil, immolated the animals sacred to the goddess with a single sweep of a long knife with a hilt of precious stones. The blood of the victims was collected preciously for curing the sick, because Mylitta extended her protection over all human weakness.

The harps, mandoras, double crystal flutes and five-stringed lyres sent swirls of harmony up to the starry vault. After having prostrated themselves, Ahmosis and Menonia mingled with the dancers, and then, detaching themselves from the coryphean group, executed their lascivious steps. Enlaced, miming the poems of amour, they delivered themselves to all the caresses of intercourse; then, after the final ecstasy, agitating flowering branches and striking silver cymbals, they celebrated the eternal triumph of Mylitta.

Elodoum, the dancer with the pale bronze body, attempted bold contortions after them, sweeping the ground with her long hair, and pirouetting with an unparalleled suppleness and agility.

Maines and Arahru then performed a kind of combat, the thrusts of which sometimes dotted the adversary's breast with pink. Uttering shrill cries, the priestesses excited them in the struggle, while the sistra, cymbals and bronze castanets resonated furiously.

Then Taina, a frail child with long nostalgic eyes, placed herself before the altar, still red with the blood of the victims, and expert jugglers threw daggers at her, the points of which fixed them in a wooden panel, forming an aureole around her head.

Himroud sang a final hymn to the goddess then, with her passionate voice, and the courtesans, enlaced, returned to the chambers of amour.

Only Ahmosis and Menonia remained on the terrace, anxious and indecisive.

"The prisons are closed at this hour," said the satrap's wife. "We couldn't return to Starzo."

"We'll liberate him tomorrow morning. In the meantime, let's take these petals, steeped in the blood of a ewe, to the goddess. You can hide under the veil of a sacrificial priestess in order to traverse the temple."

The little dancer had plunged the flowers into the crimson dew that covered the steps of the altar. She recited the prayers of hope and deliverance that disposed the Lady of Sensual Pleasure favorably to poor human beings.

Enveloped in Zazai's long veil, huddled together, they carried the branches of amour and murder religiously to the idol of the sanctuary.

XVI

BABYLON was celebrating, for the king was to preside once again over executions in the gardens of the palace. Under the porticos of temples, the priests were offering fetishes, and the fixed statues of terrible gods menaced the passers-by.

Ahmosis and Menonia, isolating themselves as much as possible, fled the brown girls with narrow foreheads and thick lips, who called to them at every street corner, to offer them barbaric jewelry, fruits or perfumes. Insults then departed from the groups of vendors, mockery and coarse jokes, to which the little courtesans paid no heed.

Curly-haired men clad in linen with woolen sleeves stopped them sometimes and embraced them violently; then, having perceived their faces under the thick veils, they insisted that they accompany them to their lodgings. They disengaged themselves with difficulty, descending narrow streets of patched and rickety houses with pink and gray terraces that seemed to be jostling one another, like the unquiet population overflowing toward the river.

"Keep your jewels clasped tight against your breast," said Menonia, anxiously.

"Oh, I've knotted them in a silk scarf."

"You know that those jewels belong to the temple and that we don't have the right to dispose of them?"

"I know that all the riches of the daughters of amour are Mylitta's."

"If the larceny is discovered we'll be subjected to the torture reserved for infidel priestesses."

Ahmosis shivered. "What is that torture, then?"

"Crucifixion. Haven't you seen the long avenue at the end of the garden, bordered by black specters, where the vultures circle night and day? All those who have stolen from the goddess are destined to die thus."

"Oh, I'm frightened!" sobbed Ahmosis. "And yet, we have no other means of conquering Starzo's guardian . . ."

"We have our beauty."

"No, no," said the young woman, with disgust. "What are you daring to propose to me? And then, the man might only be sensible to presents. But the king has given me a chest full of gold and precious stones; can I not dispose of them in order to accomplish a good deed?"

"Alas, no. Everything we possess belongs to the goddess. It's for that reason that the courtesans never quit the temple. Even when old age has withered their features and desiccated their hearts, they remain close to the idol, insensible to amorous prayers, weary and futile."

"Yes, I've seen priestesses curbed by the years, but somber veils cover their faces."

"They remain thus veiled until death, in order not to repel the worshipers of Mylitta, who only want to contemplate spring in bloom."

They had reached the temple of El Kalaieh, guarded by winged bulls with human faces—the temple of Bel mentioned by Herodotus—and they were tempted to go in.

"Can Bel not protect us against Mylitta?" asked Ahmosis, shuddering at the idea of the punishments incurred by her sin.

"Mylitta would avenge herself anyway, if it pleased her to punish us."

"What shall we do, then?"

"I don't know, but time's pressing; let's hasten to free Starzo; that's the only thing that matters, for the moment."

Having arrived at the formidable entrance to the prisons, they showed the royal seal as they had the day before. The guardian of the central dungeon was waiting for them, his face grim. He conducted them through the damp corridors to a low door that they had not noticed the previous day.

"In exchange for your riches," he said, "I'll liberate the man you're seeking."

"But what about the master's order?" said Ahmosis, timidly.

"The order isn't sufficient. You promised me presents. I want them."

Tremulously, the young woman undid the silk scarf that contained her jewels. The necklaces, clasps, belts and crowns of stones emitted a vivid radiance, seemingly animated like fiery reptiles.

With a satisfied grunt, the man plunged his hand into the treasure. Then, opening the little door, he stood aside along the wall.

Starzo was already in his friend's arms, livid and covered with wounds, but alive.

He laughed and wept by turns, unable to find words to express his delight. Almosus and Menonia embraced him passionately, intoxicated by his presence, so long desired. Mad with joy and hope, they did not hear the sniggering of the guardian, which was reverberating in the distance from the somber walls.

PART THREE

I

DUSK fell, clad in crimson and gold lace. The air palpitated with ardent odors and voluptuous breaths, carrying the soul of flowers. Since emerging from the prison, Starzo and his two companions had not quit the large garden of the temple. They gazed at one another happily, shedding their thoughts like the petals of a dream, conceiving no other joy than finding themselves together in the splendor of the sky and the vegetation in fête.

The little courtesans had given the young man perfumes and light garments. They had bandaged his wounds. And while he washed himself in the sacred pools, they were glad to set a table for him with the most delicate foodstuffs.

Menonia's eyes were shining strangely; they were the eyes of a sorceress and a priestess, illuminated by sacrificial fires. Her lips were quivering, and the blood seemed ready to spurt from their flowery calyx.

However, Starzo was only contemplating Ahmosis, the Egyptian girl, divinely beautiful under the molten sky.

"Oh," she said, "I thought I would never see you again, and I suffered a thousand deaths."

"For myself," said Menonia, "I knew full well that you would return. The goddess had promised me that."

"We were betrayed by slaves. Ahassuru recaptured all the prisoners, who have doubtless been crucified today," Starzo confirmed. "He would have besieged the temple if he had dared."

"He couldn't do anything against Mylitta!"

"The satraps are powerful. Leave the garden as little as possible."

"We only went out in order to try to find you. Now we've got you back, nothing will distract us from our amorous mission."

And in order to dissipate the clouds that had accumulated on the young man's forehead, Menonia told him how she took her friend's place at every amorous visit. The latter had, in fact, a great deal of success with the lords of Babylon, but the liberties of her lovers of an evening never surpassed the permitted limit. At the first danger, Menonia emerge from the shadow of the curtains and offered herself to the burning caresses, while Ahmosis, supple and silent, drew away secretly.

Thus, everyone was satisfied.

Starzo laughed heartily at the amorous ruse, and the satrap's wife only became dearer to him. He clasped her to his heart tenderly, seeking her lips, which she abandoned to him endlessly.

An extraordinary happiness filled their being, the ardent happiness, outside of life, which only very young people know, at the beginning of their blind tenderness.

A complete, immense beauty dissolved their souls; time no longer existed; existence appeared to them to be eternal and limitless, as to the elect of the great religions of amour. Confounded in the same intoxication, they no longer saw anything but their ecstatic eyes, disdainful of the milky azure, the stellar archipelagos of vacillating light, the fiery and aromatic breezes. They were confounded in the same ineffable dream of devouring sweetness. Tears blurred their eyes and a sob rose from their breasts.

Meanwhile, Menonia was suffering a strange anxiety, a sharp malaise that she had never felt before. The joy of the lovers was painful for her; her veins were carrying burning waves.

Indifferent to the torments of the heart, the courtesan was astonished by that novel crisis. Until then, only her senses had quivered with the joys of possession; only her ardent flesh had known the divine agony of caresses. What change was taking place within her?

"You'll never be able to belong to one another completely," she said, in a mordant voice, in order to extract them from their ecstasy. She was surprised by the wicked sentiment that had suddenly driven her to destroy their happiness.

Ahmosis and Starzo had reawakened from their common intoxication. They fixed fearful gazes upon her.

"Why those dire words?" murmured Ahmosis, reproachfully. "We were so happy!"

Menonia lowered her head, confused.

"I don't understand," said Starzo. "Can't I take my beloved away? We'll quit this land and return to Egypt, for she and I were both born on that blessed soil."

"Ahmosis has given herself to Mylitta," said the courtesan. "It's for life."

"For life!"

"Those who disobey and attempt to flee never get very far, for the people know the priestesses of pleasure. They're brought back to the temple and crucified, to be devoured by the vultures."

"Is that true?" said the terrified boatman.

"Alas," sighed Ahmosis.

"But I can take you away in my boat. I'll hide you in the reeds at the slightest danger. Who will be able to recapture you?"

"The satrap is watching. His soldiers never quit the banks of the Euphrates. They're at the gates of the city. When we were looking for you, we could never surpass a certain limit, for they would have lifted our veils and torn off our garments. We have the right to circulate in Babylon, but on the condition of returning every evening to the temple in order to accomplish our amorous mission."

"It doesn't matter," said Ahmosis. "I wouldn't attempt to run away in any case. Have I not already committed a crime against the goddess in disposing of my jewels?"

"That crime might be unknown, and the royal present can cover your larceny."

"The royal present?"

Under the interrogative gaze of her friend, Ahmosis lowered her head, trembling.

"Yes, the king came," Menonia replied, "but as always, when drunkenness troubled the visitor's senses, I replaced your lover. A coffer filled with gold and precious stones paid for the Master's fantasy."

"But the coffer belongs to you, Menonia, since it's you who gave yourself to him!" Starzo exclaimed.

"No one will ever know. I've been able to deceive the priestesses of Mylitta, but I won't deceive the goddess, who will avenge herself sooner or later," said Menonia.

"We'll appease her by means of our prayers. She's generous, she will have pity. In any case, hasn't she already protected our tenderness? She'll pardon the theft, but she couldn't pardon abandonment," Ahmosis said, sadly.

"It's to this fraud that I owe my liberty, then?" said Starzo, reproachfully.

"We had no choice of means, and you were about to die."

"It was necessary to let me suffer the fate of the other prisoners. What will my existence be henceforth, separated from you?"

"You can see one another every day," said the courtesan, "provided that you fulfill your duties with regard to Mylitta."

"And where will I find the necessary money? I'm only a poor boatman."

"You're the man I love," said Ahmosis, "and I'll give a part of the royal presents to purchase my amour. Let the wrath of the gods fall upon me!"

II

STARZO was infinitely sad. He had only recovered his lover to lose her for a second time, since the priestesses of Mylitta were consecrated to the goddess forever. What was the good of so much struggle and suffering? He remained in the arms of Ahmosis, dolorous and haggard, stammering inconsequential words, reproaches and amorous protestations.

The springs of his mentality, once courageous, broke against this final obstacle, which he had not foreseen. The abrupt comprehension of his impotence, at the very moment of triumph, was the last stroke of the bow that, in the sonorous chanterelle, broke the excessively taut string of the violin and rendered its melodious soul suddenly mute.

It would have been better for Ahmosis to have remained with the satrap, her master, than to join the sacred courtesans. Ahassuru, the cruel chief, might have been vanquished, but the goddess remained impassive and serene, mighty in all the joy that she distributed to humans.

"It's necessary to go back into the temple," said Menonia. "It's the hour of the sacrifices. They're doubtless looking for us, for the customary ceremony, for we have to dance before the altar."

Ahmosis detached herself from Starzo's arms.

"Stay in the garden, both of you," she said. "I'll be back in a moment."

The boatman did not seem to have heard his beloved, but the little courtesan shivered slightly. She was about to be able to reveal her own tenderness to the young man, for he knew full well now that she cherished him profoundly, and was suffering in seeing him belong to another.

Her flexible figure swaying softly, Ahmosis drew away along the florid avenue, bending the corollas as she passed and lifting the golden sand that fringed her veil.

As soon as she had disappeared, Menonia put her arms around Starzo's neck and glued her mouth to his feverishly.

He shuddered, and seemed to emerge from a dream. "What do you want with me?" he said.

"I love you."

"You love me? I thought you were Ahmosis' friend?"

"I'd rather be your lover." She gazed at him with eyes brilliant with passion and desire.

"But I can't love anyone but her."

"We'll hide our kisses from her. When you know my caresses, you'll no longer want to savor any others. I'm a courtesan of Mylitta, a priestess of amour, whom everyone desires. Ahmosis is only the satrap's wife; she belongs to a master and won't be able to render you happy. In any case, she's utterly ignorant of the divine ecstasy. Don't you love the passion of my lips and the savor of my kisses?"

She pressed herself against him, offering herself irresistibly. But Starzo was only thinking about his beloved, the gentle and sacred child he had always sustained and protected against life. He only saw her, unaware of the voluptuous demon who was begging for his caress.

Menonia showed him her young breasts, her pure loins, the living flood of her hair, which emitted a troubling perfume.

Starzo was prey to the cruelest of interior dramas; he remained motionless in the presence of the seductress, unable either to embrace her or to flee.

"Go away," he said finally. "Don't tempt me."

She embraced his knees, feline and undulating, and lifted her imploring hands toward him.

"I love you! Take me . . ."

She lay down in the flowers, indecent and lascivious, tearing off her veils, offering her charming body.

"I love you! Take me . . ."

She repeated the ardent phrases endlessly, and there was a great silence around them like a sort of divine elevation of beings and plants before beauty.

Ahmosis came back joyfully, with a coffer.

"This is what remains of the king's present," she said, without seeing the disturbance of the young people.

"No, no," said Starzo. "I can't accept it."

"These riches will buy my kiss. You know full well that it's necessary to make an offering to the goddess every time one possesses a temple courtesan. You're poor; how else could you acquit yourself?"

"I won't see you again. I'll depart, never to return. I'll surrender myself to the satrap."

Ahmosis uttered a cry of anguish. "You know full well that I won't be able to live henceforth without you."

"You'll forget me."

"I can't quit you!" she moaned. "Cease making me suffer, my Starzo! Every day, I'll find you again in this garden; I'll belong to you, by the will of the king, who will pay for our feast of amour. Take the chest; it contains a fortune for you, a treasure of felicity!"

"This is the property of the goddess."

"I've kept a large number of the mounts for her, and I'll have fake stones fitted to them. I'll offer them this evening, before all the assembled priestesses. No one will know that I've given you the real jewels. Only Menonia could betray us."

"I won't talk," said the courtesan, with a somber expression, "but the wrath of the gods is hanging over you."

III

IT was the evening ceremony in the temple of amour. The daughters of Mylitta prostrated themselves before the altar decorated with flowers and scintillating with precious gems under the smoke of incense and aromatics. The idol was standing on its golden pedestal, coiffed with the starry tiara; her hair descended in curly ringlets over her shoulders, which were covered by eight rows of pink pearls. The day before, the women of Babylon had come to adore the Lady of Life who watched over them. Then they had delivered themselves to prostitution, in obedience to Chaldean law, which obliged them to give themselves at least once in their life to a lover of hazard. That was to the profit of the goddess, and the returns were so considerable that no temple in the city equaled the sumptuousness of Mylitta's.

When a wife presented herself for the amorous tribute, one of the young courtesans yielded her bed to her, and everything happened for the best, in accordance with the desires of the elect. Then the honest women, having sacrificed to the goddess, returned to the conjugal penates with the just pride of a duty accomplished. Ten married women had come the day before to honor the Babylonian Venus. They were very rich and well placed individuals who had left valuable jewels and a few gold ingots.

Thanks to that munificence, the presents that Ahmosis was to bring excited less curiosity among the courtesans, but it was known that the satrap's wife had been visited by the monarch, and that supreme honor also ought to bring the temple a good dividend of riches.

After the habitual songs and dances, Ahmosis, still troubled by Starzo's kisses, advanced toward the altar. She was carrying the fake gems that she had substituted for the royal presents, and the offering seemed considerable.

She knelt down amid the vapors of sandalwood, myrrh and cinnamon, and kissed the ground at the feet of the goddess three times. Then she presented the golden basket that contained the large jewels. In the midst of rutilant stones, serpentine necklaces, turquoise and cornelian figurines, armlets and anklets that the women of Babylon had brought, Ahmosis' gift was dissimulated without difficulty.

Zazai, the High Priestess, had approached. In silence she searched the announced presents, and frowned two or three times,

"Is this really all?" she asked.

"Yes," said Ahmosis, in a faint voice.

"You swear that you haven't redirected any present?"

"I swear it."

"Get up, daughter of the temple of amour, and may Mylitta protect you."

Pale and faint, the satrap's wife mingled with the closely-packed ranks of her companions, while the songs resumed with greater force to the passionate rhythm of lyres, viols and nine-stringed harps.

The dancers launched forth, bending and straightening their supple bodies the color of yellow bronze. They writhed, arched their backs, stuck out their blooming breasts, and deployed their slender arms, seemingly beating wings like the temple pigeons.

Ahmosis and Menonia tried their savant steps in their turn. Both of them were thinking about Starzo, and their poses had a feverish languor.

The bronze cymbals and castanets became louder now, along with the plaintive sound of the stringed instruments; a kind of frenzy gripped the priestesses of amour. They snorted like ardent mares, summoning desire by means of the bracing of their back, and the harmoniously lascivious movement of their hips. They drew closer together with precise bounds, embraced momentarily, kissed one another on the lips and then, with a faint scream, drew away from one another in feigned terror, palpitating, offering themselves again and flying further apart with the regret of possession and the vehement appeal of pleasure.

That dance seemed magnificently instructive, although filled with a profound artistry. The amorousness beneath the deliberate gestures was tangible; it was the almost cruel sensuality of a woman avid with desire, palpitating with love-sickness.

On her golden throne, in the glitter of precious stones, Mylitta seemed to smile, and her emerald eyes were animated by a living spark.

Finally, drunk on perfumes, movement and perhaps remorse, Ahmosis and Menonia came to fall, swooning, at the feet of the goddess.

IV

WHEN they had danced before the idol for the triumph of amour, the little courtesans, in order to relax, played dice and consulted wooden figurines representing the beneficent or maleficent gods of Babylon. They were part-bull and part-lion, monsters with human heads and widespread wings.

Certain of those genii, whose crude representations Ahmosis caressed, hovered over the city, presiding over morbid breaths. The south-westerly wind, the most terrible, lay in ambush in the deserted quarters. The gods of fever and madness insinuated themselves into dwelling slyly and perfidiously, in order to sow desolation and death there; ghouls awaited infidel courtesans, and fleshless specters quit their tombs in order to drink the blood of thieves.

Thus, Ahmosis and Menonia were filled with dread by the evocation of those vengeful figures.

Some of the little sculpted idols that they turned over in their fingers had the feet of birds and the scales of fish; others raised the head of a vulture, a hyena a

174

wolf over the body of a dog with legs terminated by an eagle's claws. But their appearance was always frightful.

That game, known as "the game of demons" was very popular in Babylon. By practicing it with some science, one could know the good or bad events of life, the secret thoughts and projects of others—in sum, everything that it was important to know.

Ahmosis and Menonia, as they shook the dice, were thinking about their amours and asking destiny mysterious questions that chance might resolve. But the figurines remained hostile; the future, for the little courtesans, was not illuminated by any radiance.

"Oh, the goddess will avenge herself sooner or later," Ahmosis sighed.

"You've stolen, we've lied . . ."

"Amour is stronger than crime . . ."

"An amour that can never know the sweetness of liberty . . ."

"A secret voice tells me that we will be cruelly chastised."

"I know, too, that my happiness will only have an ephemeral duration. But what does it matter, if I have known the divine frisson of the body and the soul? There is no other joy on earth, and I shall depart without regret, after having lived my dream."

Menonia disposed the figurines of the redoubtable gods, moving them in accordance with the rules of the game and the combinations of chance. Ramman, with his head of a bird of prey and his wings outspread, found himself beside Zou, who unleashed the winds and the lightning.

"A man will come who will do you harm," said the courtesan.

"And that man will doubtless be the satrap, my husband, Ahassuru is like the cruel genius who scythes the crops and destroys existences."

"Ahassuru can't have pardoned you; he's doubtless waiting for an opportunity to fall upon his prey."

"Here's Lady Siris, the goddess of conspiracies, joining Zou."

The little dancer had seized a black idol aureoled with gold, whose amethyst eyes glinted slyly.

"You're forgetting to oppose to her Matou, god of war, and Barkou, master of victory. Lady Siris will be vanquished."

Laughing, Ahmosis had mixed up the idols; then, with the back of her hand, she knocked over the entire checkerboard of destiny.

"Oh! What are you doing?" Menonia protested.

"I prefer not to know. What point is there in veiling the brightness of my sky? If the star of life is only to shine for me for a few short hours, at least let its radiance warm me without any obstacle."

"Personally, I prefer to know the future. One is stronger when one has an enemy to fight who shows himself."

"Oh! Do you believe this oracle to be infallible?"

"It has never deceived me. I affirm to you, Ahmosis, that a great danger is threatening us. Perhaps the satrap whom you fled is advancing on Babylon to destroy the temple."

"He's under the king's orders, and must obey him."

"It's said that the king is having hallucinations that are troubling his reason. Might he not order our death in a moment of dementia?"

But Ahmosis had risen to her feet. "Oh, let's not think about these things. Starzo will come, and I have a joyful heart. Don't spoil that adorable day for me."

The satrap's wife had put flowers in her hair. She was almost naked; her eyes were shining between the antimony lines of her eyelids. She quit her friend and her veil, lifted by the rapidity of her course, rose up over her elegant legs, over her rounded thighs, muscular and strong.

Sighing, Menonia resumed the game of fateful figurines.

V

SINCE the massacre of the guards and the eunuchs, Ahassuru, the cruel satrap, had, indeed, only been thinking about vengeance. No desire troubled his heart for the fugitive wives, but he wanted to recapture them in order to subject them to the most frightful tortures.

The passionate subtleties that tempt and madden the powerful of the earth, the homicidal perversities, the dissolute sensual pleasures that they seek, create within them a sort of feverish atmosphere, which they want to enjoy as much as the material form of their covetousness.

All women, for the tyrant, were victims or instruments of pleasure, who passed through the practical monotony of his appetites like the ghouls of legend through the flames of the pyre. He had committed all sins, all murders and all lusts. His hands were red with blood and his soul black with sin; so he thought with intoxication about the moment of satisfaction.

Since a slave had come to warn him, tremulously, that his faithful guardians were being massacred and that his wives were fleeing, Ahassuru had no longer had any enthusiasm for the distractions of war. He was camped outside Babylon with his troops, indifferent to the orders of Nabuchodonosor, who was said, in any case, to be attacked by a strange illness.

The prophet had predicted to the king, after the capture of Jerusalem, that Yahveh, the god of the Jews, would punish him cruelly, and the prediction was in the process of being realized. The powerful monarch of Babylon and Nineveh had extended his conquests everywhere, beating Necho at Circesium, reducing King Sedecias to slavery,[1] laying siege to the city of Tyr, subjugating Egypt, which had assured him an enormous booty, and taking his arms as far as Spain. Proud of so much success, he had wanted to be adored, but Yahveh, in order to confound his pride, had disturbed his reason. His madness was not continuous, but it extended its dark wings over him for an hour or two almost every day.

The satraps thus remained masters of the realm, conserving all military authority, and, the satrapies being small in number, the chiefs of those domains amassed enormous riches and exercised a redoubtable authority.

If he had dared, Ahassuru would have overturned the temple of Mylitta, in which the infidel wives had taken refuge, some time ago, but the goddess inspired a superstitious terror in him. It was said that the Lady of Sensual Pleasure was invincible, and those who were reckless enough to combat her perished in the most horrible torments.

---

1 Sedecias is a Latinized form of Zedekiah; he was the last king of Juda prior to its destruction by the Babylonians.

After the periodic wars, the execution of prisoners recurred monotonously in the history of the four Empires. Cuneiform inscriptions inform us, after the lapse of so many centuries, of the massacres and tortures of those barbaric peoples, and threaten with the most terrible punishments anyone who attempts to destroy that evidence of the grandeur of kings.

Mylitta, the Lady of Amour, the Babylonian Venus, presided over the tortures. The golden statue dominated the crowd of prisoners in her serene glory; she protected the Chaldean chiefs in particular, and it was for that reason that Ahassuru dared not attack the temple of the goddess.

Ready for any event, he remained at the gates of the city, hoping that some maleficent intervention might deliver Himroud and Ahmosis to him.

Around him, the executioners were preparing their instruments of torture: scissors to cut the skin into thin strips, pincers to prize the eyes out of their orbits, ropes, saws and hatchets. Tortured prisoners were finishing dying on the stakes and crosses that formed long funereal lines to either side of the camp. That spectacle rejoiced the heart of the tyrant.

VI

THE temple was packed with the crowd of the gallant, with complicated adornments, long robes embroidered with silken designs and fringed with multicolored pearls. Thick frizzy hair was adorned with pointed or square bonnets, in accordance with the importance of the sumptuous lords.

Many of them coveted Ahmosis, the prettiest of the dancers of Mylitta, and brought her rich presents, but Starzo always triumphed with regard to his friend. It was to the humble boatman that the sighs, the kisses and the caresses went, for him that all the amorous flowers of that adorable spring bloomed.

"My Starzo," said the satrap's wife, "I had not lived before knowing the sweetness of your embrace, and I could no longer exist if it were necessary to renounce seeing you. I want to ignore the king himself, who obtained your presence for me, and who has deigned to cross the threshold of my chamber again."

Once again the young man's eyebrows furrowed.

"The king has come?"

"Yes, but you know very well that he has only possessed my shadow. As always, another has taken my place."

"Menonia?"

"Menonia, whose heart is free, and who gives herself at her whim."

Starzo remembered the feverish words of the courtesan, who had already offered herself to him several times.

"Menonia doesn't love anyone, you say?"

"No," said Ahmosis, laughing. "Why ask that question?"

"Because Memonia is beautiful and equally worthy of inspiring a profound amour."

"She has certainly been cherished by many of the lords of Babylon, and her senses have vibrated under savant caresses. I don't believe her to be insensible to eulogies, nor to the fêtes of the flesh, but her soul, I repeat, scorns the joys of her body."

Starzo did not reply. He held his mistress against his breast and intoxicated himself with amour. Everything that was not the present felicity no longer existed for him.

The young people formed a charming couple. No ancient statues ever offered a more complete harmony of forms. Their heads seemed to go to sleep in their voluptuous ecstasy; their eyelids, fringed by long lashes, allowed eyes moist with slaked tenderness to gleam between their somber lines; their thin and delicate noses with quivering nostrils had an Egyptian purity; their lips delicately modeled, retained a smile full of gentleness, melancholy and charm.

In truth, Starzo and Ahmosis resembled one another strangely. The distinction of their narrow hands and feet, the suppleness of their figure, the roundness of their long legs with harmoniously modeled ankles belonged to a distant and mysterious race, surely to a very ancient and aristocratic family.

Lying among the flowers, they loved one another without restraint, until the hour when the sun tinted the languishing leaves with crimson and gold.

In that part of the garden, reserved for the high priestess, no one came to disturb them. Only Menonia, parting the branches cautiously, sometimes gazed at them silently, and an expression of dolorous jealousy contorted her features. But the lovers, lost in their dream, did not see her; they only had attention and desire for one another.

"When I was little," said Ahmosis, "I lived in a sumptuous and charming palace. The open porticos were supported by light columns crowned by a lotus flower. Large onyx vases presented embalmed vegetal spays that were renewed every day."

"Yes," said Starzo," I've seen a similar palace in my infancy. The walls bore brilliant paintings, and in the courtyard there was a deep pool where I used to sail papyrus boats."

Ahmosis clapped her hands joyfully. "That's it, my beloved! We certainly lived in the same city."

The young man's face darkened. "It was a long time ago, but my memories are very precise. When I close my eyes, I can see all the landscapes that enchanted my first dreams."

"Personally, I've forgotten. It's as if those things are surrounded by a cloud. Sometimes, a clear patch forms, but then everything falls back into shadow again."

"I don't want to integrate the past. It's too cruel and it torments me pointlessly. I'll never see my family again, who doubtless died in captivity. It's a miracle that I escaped the carnage."

"I learned, by virtue of vague confidences on the part of Morphy, the old witch who brought me up, that I was born on the banks of the Nile, and that soldiers carried me away in order to sell me to the nomads who followed the conquering troops. A sun-tanned woman had put me in a piece of cloth in order to hide me from other covetous individuals. I know, by virtue of a fetish that was found on me, which I wore for a long time, that I'm of illustrious birth."

"Ah," said Starzo, "we're from the same land of sun and amour, and it's for that reason that our hearts have fused together in an ineffable tenderness."

"We'll belong to one another until death."

"Until death," repeated the young man, gluing his mouth recklessly to that of his Beloved.

VII

MENONIA felt her amour for the handsome boatman increasing, and suffered in silence. She had never experienced anything similar. It was a delectable and terrible sickness that left her body and soul broken. In everything that surrounded her, in everything that she saw, she rediscovered the anguishing obsession. Her memories were strangely animated; a passionate breath made her heart palpitate, bewildered by tenderness and desire. To the mysterious charm of her covetousness she added the infinity of her dreams.

The sight of her friend's happiness troubled her infinitely, but she could not help spying on the lovers, in order to watch their embraces and their kisses. Her blood seethed more forcefully then, and she would have given her life for an hour of similar felicity.

"O divinity of glory and amour," she sighed, while decorating with fateful branches a little altar of Mylitta of which she was especially fond, "be propitious for me; charm the heart of the man I love!"

She prayed for a long time before the goddess, and then returned to the terrace in order to obey her voluptuous mission. The lords of Babylon disputed her favors, and she also had to replace Ahmosis, who did not want to betray her dear Starzo. After so many embraces, hoping to have mastered her body, she closed her eyes on her ravaged couch, summoning sleep; but repose did not come, for the demon of amour was within her, like a hornet in the heart of a rose.

Sometimes, to calm her burning flesh, Menonia went down into the temple and lay down at the foot of the idol, amid the flowers and the perfumes. She gazed at the little lamp that burned night and day before the golden statue. Her eyes, widened by passion, lingered hypnotically on the breast of Mylitta, scintillating with a blaze of precious stones.

The desire took her to snatch the necklaces, the amulets, the clasps and the precious plaques in order to pay for Starzo's kisses in her turn. But the young man would doubtless reject her with horror after such a sacrilege. He would not accept from Menonia what he had tolerated on the part of Ahmosis.

After those culpable thoughts, the little courtesan sobbed for hours, asking the pardon of the goddess for her unworthiness. She prostrated herself fervently, renewing her vow of fidelity and obedience, promising, in a surge of her entire being, to devote herself eternally to the divinity of amour.

"What do you do, Ahmosis," she asked her companion, "to have that new and radiant beauty?"

"I'm beloved," replied the satrap's wife.

"And what are the philters that give you the magical power to please the elect of your soul? The men who possess me leave me indifferent, while I can't charm the one I desire."

"It's necessary to pray to Mylitta."

"The goddess doesn't deign to listen to me."

"Perhaps it's because your wishes are too ambitious."

"The man I love is the humblest of all those who solicit my favors!"

Ahmosis laughed, not divining, in her imprudent confidence, that Menonia wanted Starzo's caresses. The sometimes-hateful gaze of her companion did not put her on guard, so blind does happiness render those it covers with its golden veil.

"Let's pray together for the triumph of your dream."

"Let's pray fervently, yes, let's pray again."

Narrowly enlaced, mingling the silky curls of their hair, they knelt down in the temple at the very moment when Starzo came to take his lover away to dangerous ecstasy.

Every day he bought one of the gems that the little courtesan had given him to pay for his happiness. Zazai, the High Priestess, received the amorous offerings without suspecting the larceny.

After all, Ahmosis thought, *we're making restitution to the goddess of what we have taken from her, and the crime isn't so great.*

The treasure, however, was diminishing, and the lovers thought with terror about the moment when it would be necessary to procure other resources.

"What will we do, my beloved, when none of the royal offering remains any longer?"

"We'll run away," said Ahmosis, resolutely.

"That's death, as you know very well."

"Better to die than not to see one another any longer."

"Certainly! Better to die!" Starzo rolled his forehead against the young woman's breast, intoxicating himself on her kisses and her perfume. "Your caresses are sweeter than milk and honey. Let me live my dream until the supreme moment of the separation."

"Here are my lips and my kiss, here is my flesh and the best of my being. There is not one place on my body that isn't yours."

"Your loins are as pure as the curve of a precious vase. Your hands and feet are made to bear the glory of bracelets and rings. Your breast is the cup of intoxication where my mouth slakes its thirst infinitely, and I adore the double colonnette of your legs with reflections of rosy amber."

Ahmosis passed her frail fingers through her lover's hair.

"You're beautiful, my adored! Your eyes are as profound as sacred lakes, and your arms, more flexible than the stem of a palm tree, fill me with delights. Hold me tightly against you, in order that I might enter entirely into your heart."

Faint with jealousy, Menonia listened to the lovers, and their inflamed words were as many blades lacerating her breast. She had never known a similar torture, and she did not think anyone could suffer more. Feverish and anguished, she hid in the bushes every day in order to listen to the amorous litany. Her eyes fascinated by the cherished image, her soul chilled by an untranslatable distress, she prolonged her torment until the moment of adieux. Then, invisible and obstinate, she followed the couple, who went back up to the terraces, and exhaled their tenderness once more beneath the starry sky.

Menonia let herself slide to the ground in order to weep at her ease, but a sudden revolt soon obliged her to get up, her mouth contorted and her gaze hateful.

She prowled in the gardens, and went down as far as the river, dreaming about terrible and refined vengeances. The most contrary impressions were born within her, succeeding one another, exasperating her morbid sensitivity. Knowing that she was so alone in the world, her heart swelled and filled with sorrow. She thought that she would never awaken anything but the vile and ephemeral desire of the human beast, that any ideal of sentiment was forbidden to her; and, again, with her forehead in her clenched fists, she wept bitterly.

VIII

"HERE, take it . . ."
        "What is it?"
"The treasure of the goddess! I too have stolen it for you, and I'm rich now! I can buy your kiss like Ahmosis!"

Menonia threw a fistful of rutilant gems on to Starzo's knees: the pearls, rubies and emeralds of Mylitta.

"What have you done?" said the young man, fearfully. "You have to take these jewels back."

"No, no, never. I've stolen them for you."

"But I don't want them."

"Ahmosis despoiled the goddess in the same way, and you accepted her presents."

"Amour triumphed over my scruples. I'm no less culpable of it, and I await the punishment."

"Yes, you were in love. You still are, and you disdain me."

"I have a sincere amity for you."

"Nothing more?"

Starzo kept silent, incapable of disguising his thought. However, he experienced an indefinable sensation of stupor and overwhelming pity. He had stood up, and pushed away the jewels, which had fallen to the ground, with his foot.

"Pick that up," he said, "and take it back to the temple before the evening ceremony. No one might be aware of your larceny yet."

With a cry of rage, the little courtesan put the marvelous gems in a flap of her veil, and drew away at a run.

The boatman sighed profoundly; he would have liked to express to his friend, who finally joined him, what he felt, infinitely tender and also infinitely cruel; but a superstitious dread paralyzed his brain, and he was only able to stammer: "Oh, my beloved, you were right; It will soon be necessary to flee."

"Yes, yes, I knew that," said Ahmosis. "Existence here is no longer possible."

"You can hide in my boat, and we'll try to escape the surveillance on the banks. The reeds are dense. I know inviolable shelters."

"When shall we leave, my beloved."

"As soon as my preparations are concluded."

"Is some danger threatening us?"

"Perhaps. Don't you have any fear, then?"

"What fear could I have, while you're beside me?"

By virtue of a scruple of delicacy, Starzo did not want to reveal to his lover the pursuit of which he was the object. He was reluctant to denounce Menonia's treason.

"Our resources will soon be exhausted," he said, sadly. "Then it will be separation."

"What if I presented myself to the king? Perhaps he'd consent to return to the temple?"

"Shut up! I forbid you to evoke those memories."

Instead of finding an appeasement in his amour, the young man's nerves were taut, to the point that a real physical suffering was added to his mental suffering. Away from his lover, he no longer slept; a sudden exasperation sometimes threw him out of his bed, and he spent his nights walking in front of the terraces of the temple, his heart swollen by a somber anxiety.

It was decided that they would leave during the great festival of the goddess, after the sacred dances. The temple being full of people, it would be easy to slip away in disguise and reach the water-gate.

Drunk with joy, Ahmosis made her confidences to Menonia the same evening, not suspecting that she was dooming herself irremediably by so doing.

The little courtesan went pale with emotion.

"You're going away, then?" she said, in a tremulous voice.

"Yes."

"Forever?"

"Forever."

"What about me?"

"You? You'll stay, since you've devoted yourself freely to the cult of Mylitta. You'll pray for the success of our enterprise."

"You're going to death!"

"Perhaps..."

"How can you struggle against the satrap's troops?"

"We won't struggle."

"You'll be tortured!"

"May the Lady of Amour protect us."

"But I don't want you to go!"

"You don't want it?" Surprised, Ahmosis raised a beautiful, honest and tender gaze upon her friend.

"You mustn't leave," said Menonia, stammering. "Aren't you happy in our midst? Why seek danger? And then, I have your secret ..."

"Oh! You wouldn't betray me!" said the young woman, with a beautiful, confident smile. "I know that your heart is incapable of such a black thought."

"Someone might divine what I don't say."

"A double reason for leaving. Starzo and I will follow the banks of the Euphrates. My beloved knows all the hiding-places in the vegetation, the dense nests of reeds where men could live, unknown to anyone. We'll flee after the ceremony on the day of the goddess."

Angrily, Menonia ripped her veil. "Go, then!" she said, in a low voice, "and may your destiny be accomplished."

IX

THE little courtesan had interrogated the sacred figurines, and the oracle of the divinities, again, had predicted death. Ahmosis had to die, therefore, since she had rendered her friend's heart desperate. Menonia was accustomed to seeing her close to her, so gentle, so tender and so pretty. Into the feverish life of the daughter of Mylitta she brought a little of the serene and appeasing clarity of her soul. There were moments when, in spite of her jealousy, it did her good to rest her eyes on that chaste and childlike grace.

The departure of the lovers took all joy and all courage from her, for it was not only an exquisite companion that she was losing but a certain lover, the only man that she had loved since entering the temple. Tender thoughts were succeeded by thoughts of hatred; a bitter desire for vengeance caused the courtesan's entire body to tremble, writhing in unspeakable torments.

Every day, meanwhile, she brought the young couple palm liquor in a precious vase, and the temptation came to her to poison that beverage, which she alone prepared, having solicited the favor of serving her friend from the outset.

The festival of the goddess was approaching; it was important to act rapidly. Menonia waited for the decisive moment in an intolerable anxiety. Certainly, she would rather kill Ahmosis than know that she was happy somewhere else with Starzo. Perhaps the latter would come back to her when the influence of another had ceased to numb him in a detestable intoxication.

All through the day that preceded the crime she was overexcited, strange and incomprehensible. She was dismayed, breathless, disturbed by the most ardent desire and the most mystical dream, precipitated from summits haunted by celestial birds into the mire where filthy beasts wallowed. It was a nameless torture that retained her in her room, shaken by sobs and gasps.

Finally, she mixed with the wine of forgetfulness the venomous plants that put one to sleep for eternity, promising herself only to fill one cup and to break the vase when Starzo wanted to drink in his turn.

She disposed honey cakes and fruits in a basket, and then headed lightly toward the gardens where the amorous couple took refuge every day.

The satrap's wife was the first to perceive her friend.

"Be welcome, Menonia; you have not forgotten those whom joy makes thirsty, and who have only been living on kisses for hours."

"Drink," said the courtesan, presenting the young woman with a cup filled with a liquid with amethyst reflections.

Ahmosis extended her hand toward the sweet beverage. "Will Starzo not have his share?"

"Drink first; I've only brought one cup, supposing that it would be sufficient for your tenderness."

But Ahmosis shook her head, smiling. "I desire my beloved to put his lips where I shall put mine; the wine of forgetfulness will seem better to me thus."

Starzo leaned toward his lover, but the courtesan overturned the liquid abruptly, which spread over the roses. Then the precious vase broke in her hands, which bled.

"Clumsy!" she said. "I've lost the wine and injured myself."

Tearing off a fragment of her veil, Ahmosis immediately tried to bandage her friend, who was sobbing recklessly, her face tilted over her shoulder

There was now a great disturbance in her heart. She allowed herself to be cared for, like a little girl, glad to feel Starzo's fingers running over her arm, for he knew how to cure deep wounds. With infinite precaution, he wrapped the light fabric around the dolorous hand and stemmed the blood that was flowing in thin trickles.

Menonia, her soul filled with intoxication, inhaled the perfume of wilting flowers, and the odor of the sap of soft new shoots, around which golden insects were maneuvering.

There was a peace in that place so complete that one might have thought that human misery had never dared to cross the threshold of that paradise. In spite of the seething of her hatred and her desire, the courtesan recognized the power of divine nature, the immemorial beauty of things unsullied by the wickedness of people.

X

"MORPHY, I've come to consult your science."
They were in the lair of the sorceress, at the end of a black and sordid street.

The old woman was crouching over a piece of cloth, and a child nearby was weaving flowery branches.

"What do you want with me, priestess of Mylitta?"

"I want to talk to you about Ahmosis, whom you brought up and gave to the satrap Ahassuru."

"Ahmosis was sold at auction on the terrace of the temple. She was subject to the fate of the daughters of Babylon. I don't have to account for her existence."

"I know that," said Menonia. "You acted in accordance with your conscience, so it isn't a reproach that I'm addressing to you."

"What do you desire, then?"

Morphy had risen to her feet painfully, and stared at the courtesan with the round eyes of a bird of prey.

"Ahmosis has quit the satrap."

"Yes, she's with you in the temple of Mylitta."

"She's going to leave."

"With Starzo, whom she loves. Her designs are known to me." The old woman laughed cruelly, uncovering her black gums.

"Can't you do anything to stop her?"

"Nothing."

"However, if I were to give you my jewels . . ."

"Your jewels belong to the goddess."

"I've despoiled her for you. Here's a necklace of cornelian and turquoise; here are gold rings and cameos." Menonia uncovered a scintillation of gemstones in a corner of her veil.

"Aha! You too are a thief!"

With a fearful gaze, the courtesan pointed at the child, who continued to assemble her flowers.

"That's Penhoe, my second daughter, the one who has replaced Ahmosis. She's not from this country and doesn't know our language. There's no danger of treason."

"Since you read my soul so well," said Menonia, "do you know what brings me here?"

"I know it."

"Well, in exchange for the jewels, do you want to help me make Starzo love me?"

"That's not in my power. But I know a secret that will fill you with ease."

"Quickly, confide it to me."

Morphy put her crooked finger into the pile of gemstones. "You know that you're risking your life by despoiling the goddess?"

"I don't care about life, and I'd abandon it for an hour of amour. Tell me your secret."

The old woman put the gems in a safe place; then she took two amulets from her bosom, engraved with hieroglyphic inscriptions.

"These," she said "are what Ahmosis and Starzo were wearing when they were stolen during the Egyptian campaign."

"These stones are similar."

"Have you not noticed the resemblance between the lovers?"

"Yes," said Menonia, her soul filled with a sudden light. And she added, effortfully, frightened by what she was about to say: "Starzo is Ahmosis' brother?"

"Yes."

"And you haven't informed those culpable children?"

"What would be the point? It's necessary not to oppose the will of the gods."

After an anguished silence, Menonia said, timidly: "These fetishes have no value; give them to me."

The old woman laughed nastily. "Take them," she said, "but you won't prevent the sinister oracle from being realized. The wrath of Bel is hanging over the temple of Mylitta."

The courtesan drew away at a run. She had obeyed a mysterious power, a sort of perverse instinct, in going to interrogate Morphy, the child-stealer, the maleficent sorceress. And she saw again, in an obscure distance, where vague forms were swarming, the wretched woman caring away two little beings in her black arms, Morphy had abandoned the boy, or had sold him to the boatmen of Babylon, reserving Ahmosis in order

199

to draw more ample profits from her. The brother and sister had found one another again, and loved one another, without suspecting their common origin; but the same amorous blood ran within them; heating their generous soul and puerile imagination.

Starzo, older and more robust than Ahmosis, had been happy to make use of his strength in favor of the little girl's debility; he had welcomed the impulses of that compressed and plaintive soul, and had conquered her nostalgic gaze, which clung desperately to the caressant flight of birds in order to rise with them into the sunlight and infinite space. Although she was pained by the injustice of fate, having always suffered, Ahmosis had affectionate and gentle words for her friend. But her smile hid many tears: tears of desire, dread and hope; tears prettier than dewdrops in the calices of flowers. Infinitely tender and more refined than pauper girls of her own age, she was incessantly wounded by the rudeness of beings and the coarseness of sentiments. Without wishing for a higher existence, she had wanted more bounty and nobility around her.

The violent and despotic Morphy maltreated the child when she had not brought back the habitual income. Sly, cantankerous and cruel, she only took pleasure in tormenting others. She had terrible fits of anger, which left her breathless and exhausted, but not disarmed. And all of Ahmosis' chagrin gave rise to interminable confidences, to which Starzo listened, sitting on a step of the quay beside the little girl, whom he warmed with his caresses.

Life had gone by in that chaste intimacy. Ahmosis had become a marvelous flower of beauty and Starzo had conquered rights to the admiration of the virgins of Babylon. But the amorous couple had only had eyes for one another, unable to conceive of any other tenderness.

Grimly, Menonia told herself those things, and her jealous soul swelled with bitterness.

XI

THE courtesan had traversed the old quarters of Babylon, ripening malevolent projects, for, more than ever, her desire went toward Starzo, the lover of another and the only beloved. She experienced an ardent impulsion toward evil, an awakening of perverse instincts so sudden and so formidable that it annihilated her better resolutions in an instant.

And then, Starzo was no longer the obscure Euphrates boatman; his illustrious birth gave him a new attraction. What woman would not have been proud to press him against her heart? Already, certainly, he had strength and beauty, but that prestige of race rendered him infinitely seductive.

Men stopped in Menonia's passage and tried to lift her veil.

"Where are you going, imprudent girl?"

"Is it to crime or amour?"

"One only hides oneself so well in order to accomplish a culpable action."

She struggled angrily and fled without responding to the gallant queries.

Brown women with narrow foreheads and thick lips offered themselves to the men she had disdained.

"We're prettier than that child, and we don't put on fancy airs!" Those prowlers of the suburbs were clad in garish fabrics; their flesh emitted a strong odor of cosmetics and vulgar essences.

Menonia went down a narrow street bordered with rickety houses with pink terraces. The shops, decorated with faience plaques, had been closed for a long time, and the lower part of the constructions, coated with red ocher, was barely distinguishable. Figures of goddesses and gods standing on their sacred animals—lions or bulls—were still receiving the offerings of their worshipers, guided by little horn lamps that were burning on the pedestals.

The priestess of amour was returning to the temple of Mylitta by way of long detours, in order to avoid the suspicion of anyone who might have followed her. The banks of the Euphrates, which she finally reached, were not presented, like those of the Nile, under the aspect of grandiose constructions announcing to the world the activity of a powerful and laborious people. Baked or enameled brick and layers of dried reeds formed the principal elements of houses and temples in that backward part of the city.

Soon, soldiers assembled before stairways carved into the rock, blocks of limestone and profound flints, barred her passage. They too wanted to embrace her and profit from her youth and beauty.

She defended herself desperately, frightened to find herself so far from the temple, for she no longer recognized her route.

"Leave me alone," she said. "I'm a priestess of Mylitta."

The men laughed coarsely. "Better to stay with us, beauty. The temple isn't safe for the daughters of amour."

"The temple isn't safe?"

"Listen," said a soldier, obliging her to sit down beside him on a heap of stones. "We're at the satrap's orders and we're going to ensure his vengeance."

"What vengeance?"

"Ahassuru's two wives are under the protection of Mylitta. It's Mylitta who must perish, with all her courtesans."

"And in what manner are we to succumb?"

"By fire."

"Ah!" said Menonia, ironically. "Haven't you thought that I might betray your plans? You're very imprudent to tell me these things."

"You're free to betray us; nothing can save you, for the people are with us."

"What about the king?"

"The king is a prisoner in his palace. Don't you know that he's mad?"

"Mad?"

"Yes, since his visit to the temple of amour. It's Mylitta who has cast the spell on him, hence the anger of the gods against the goddess."

"It isn't Mylitta who doomed the king; it's Yahweh, the god of the Jews, who condemned him, to avenge his prophets. He's attracted celestial anger to us. Jeremiah, as you know, has cursed the Chaldeans. Joachim,[1] the

---

1 Joachim is a Latin form of Jehoiakim the king of Juda from 608-598 B.C. The account of Nebuchadnezzar ordering his body to be

204

king of Jerusalem, was to perish in the battle and his body remain without sepulcher. Nabuchodonosor had the treasures of the Jewish temple brought to Babylon; it's that crime that haunts him, to the point of troubling his reason."

"I know, said the soldier pensively, "that the body of Joachim, murdered by order of our king, was thrown before the walls without burial, but the Chaldean people don't want to believe in the resentment of the god of Israel. It's Mylitta they accuse. The satraps have surrounded Babylon with their troops; they alone are masters of the city."

"Oh," said Menonia, "the people love the goddess of amour; they wouldn't attack her altars. Let them recall the massacres in Jerusalem and the tortures of Sedecias, and they'll have the explanation of the anger of Israel. The prediction of the prophets is realized! Our king will be expelled from the company of men and his body will be soaked by the dew of heaven."

"Perhaps. In the meantime, the satraps dictate their laws and act as they wish. Stay with us, child, and no harm will come to you."

"No," said Menonia. "I want to return to the temple and die with my companions."

"Why die? Life reserves long happy days for you."

"Oh, you don't know," she said. "I too have a vengeance to accomplish. Afterwards, death will be sweet for me."

---

thrown down outside the walls of the city comes from Josephus. Between Jehoiakim's reign and that of Zedekiah, his son Jeconiah, or Jehoiachin, succeeded him for three months, but does not figure in the present account.

She had slipped through the arms of the half-drunken man, and she ran way along the river, guided by the lights of the temple, which she perceived in the distance.

"Bah!" said the soldier, bursting into laughter. "We'll soon have all the priestesses of Mylitta, and we can scorn the kisses of that girl."

XII

FURTIVELY, Menonia traversed the temple and regained her room. Exhausted by fatigue, she let herself fall on to her bed, and reflected feverishly on the night's events. Life had scarcely commenced for her, and her soul was already heavier with sin and charged with more iniquities than those of the conquerors of Babylon.

She had lied, stolen from the goddess and betrayed her best friend. Her flesh burning with culpable desires, she had wanted to kill everything that was most dear to her in the world, and in spite of her faults, her thoughts were taking pleasure in the evocation of a crime more frightful than everything she had done thus far.

Alone with her conscience, she recalled all the perverse imaginations and all the secret shame with which she had soiled herself. She tore at her heart with her fingernails, in order to make the red and dolorous tears flow, in order to hollow out more profoundly the wounds by which she was agonizing. An anguish gripped her throat, an unknown suffering that she increased with delight.

So, in a matter of days deliverance would come, with the annihilation of the temple of amour and its courtesans. All of them would perish, since that was the will of the people.

From being bitter and vengeful, her thoughts became mild and compassionate. Tears ran down her cheeks, moistening her tremulous hands. But she made the resolution to keep her secret, to leave her companions in their serene confidence. Yes, it would be good to disappear thus, in a glorious apotheosis. The daughters of amour would be consumed by the sacred fire; their limbs would be twisted in the immense hearth, which would light up the sky with a single jet.

Until morning, Menonia evoked the terrible and grandiose vision, already sensing the flames caressing her ardent flesh, rolling her in their capricious waves, and she felt herself possessed by the reckless ecstasy of martyrs.

When she went down into the temple, a luminous peace illuminated her face. She prostrated herself before the altar of the goddess, offering her imminent torture to her in expiation of the sins that she had committed.

For three days she kept her secret, always hoping that the enemy would destroy the temple; but on the morning of the third day, as she traversed the temple, Ahmosis, full of joy, told her that her flight was decided, and that she would meet Starzo that evening.

A flood of blood rose to the courtesan's face. "You can't see Starzo again," she said, violently.

"Why?" asked Ahmosis, shivering. "Have I been wrong, then, to confide in you? I thought you were my best friend."

"It's because I'm your friend that I want to prevent that crime."

"A crime, you say? I don't understand."

Menonia took from her bosom the two amulets that Morphy had given her.

"Oh!" said the satrap's wife. "That's a jewel similar to the one I once wore . . ."

"Look carefully, and recognize this fetish, which reposed on your infantile breast, and which doubtless protected you during your infancy."

"I see . . ." said Ahmosis. "One of these fetishes was mine . . . but the other?"

"The other belonged to Starzo . . . to your brother, Starzo. Do you understand now why you can't flee with the man you love?"

Ahmosis, fainting, stared at her companion with eyes widened by surprise and joy.

"My brother, you say?"

"Yes, Starzo is your brother. Morphy stole both of you during the Egyptian war; it's from her that I obtained this sad secret."

But the satrap's wife embraced Menonia tenderly. "Thank you," she said, "for what you've just told me. I'm glad, to the utmost depths of my soul."

"Glad? But isn't it the most frightful of crimes to belong to one's brother?"

"Here, perhaps," said Ahmosis, "but not in my homeland, where the children of Pharaohs are united in order to keep their divine blood pure. In the same way, in the great Egyptian families, the daughters marry their brothers; you see that I'm an example of my race.

Moreover, Starzo and I have seen and recognized one another. Nothing in the world could disunite us!"

Menonia had never suffered as much. So her rival would be happy, in spite of all the obstacles. Not only would she escape the wrath of the gods, but a long existence of joy and amour would be her share when, delivered from all pursuit, she and her beloved would attain the marvelous shores of her beloved homeland.

The courtesan's arteries were throbbing more forcefully. It seemed that the ground was vanishing beneath her feet. Closing her eyes to the splendors that surrounded her, she buried herself in a frightful interior vision without trying to react against the jealousy that possessed her despotically. The morbid seizure became painful to the point of malaise and delirium.

"Come," she said, "let's go back into the temple."

"Why? The ceremony is concluded; all our companions are on the terraces." She indicated the priestesses of Mylitta, who were playing a multitude of charming games, laughing and capricious.

"Come," said Menonia. "I want to tell you, before the goddess, what I have in my heart."

"But Starzo is going to come."

"He'll find you at the foot of the altar. Come, I tell you."

Devoid of suspicion, Ahmosis followed her friend.

A ray of sunlight penetrated through a stained-glass rose-window, traversed the nave and came to illuminate the faces of the two women; but suddenly, a cloud passed, veiling the sky, and all joy disappeared.

"What do you want with me?" asked Ahmosis, anxiously.

"What I have to tell you will doubtless cause you great pain."

"Speak without dread." She squeezed her friend's cold hand, seeking to comprehend.

"Swear to me before the goddess not to leave this evening."

Ahmosis rebelled. "No," she said, firmly. "I can't promise you that."

"Then one of us must die," said Menonia, tremulously. She had thrown weapons down in front of Ahmosis. "Choose, and defend yourself," she murmured, her lips livid and her gaze crazed,

"You want to kill me? Why?"

"Because I love Starzo! Do you understand?"

"You love him? But do you not have all the powerful men in Babylon? What can the love of a simple boatman matter to you?"

"I love him; that's sufficient," she repeated, with a passionate obstinacy.

Ahmosis had picked up a weapon, but, taking her friend's murderous gesture for a game, she parried weakly, and turned her gaze incessantly toward the entrance to the sanctuary in the hope of seeing her lover appear.

The blades gleamed; already, crimson droplets were gliding over Ahmosis' breast.

"This is serious, then?" she said.

With one bound, Menonia threw herself upon her companion.

The blades dug into flesh now, and emerged red at each of the combatants' embraces. The two women were no longer speaking, their lips taut and their hearts breathless.

But Ahmosis threw away her weapon and folded her arms. "I won't defend myself any more," she said, disdainfully. "Strike me, then, since that's your will." She had seen Starzo enter, and all her anger had disappeared.

"Starzo!" groaned Menonia, falling to her knees.

Distraught, the young man advanced toward the two women.

"You're wounded? What is it, then? Why this fight, this fury?"

"Starzo," said Menonia, sobbing, "don't curse me! I alone am guilty, and I ought to expiate . . ."

"She loves you," said Ahmosis. "Choose between her and me."

"No, no," cried the courtesan, "you know full well that your lover cherishes you profoundly and uniquely. Anything he could say would wound me even more cruelly. Don't speak, Starzo; I know the invincible sentiment that animates you; I know that no tenderness is worth as much to you as that of Ahmosis." And as the young man remained silent, she sighed. "Oh, I hoped, in spite of myself, that a word of pity might escape your lips, that you might experience a little commiseration for one who is about to disappear and who, in spite of her sins, has only known one amour."

Starzo approached the courtesan in order to take away the weapon that she was pressing against her breast, but she drove it violently into her bosom and collapsed, with a sigh, on the steps of the altar.

"Listen," she murmured, in a hoarse voice, to the lovers, who were weeping convulsively. "Just now I wanted to prevent you from escaping, to keep you near me and die with you, but now I'm telling you that you must leave Babylon as quickly as possible, for your existence is in peril. The satrap is going to set fire to the temple of Mylitta. Tomorrow, it might be too late. Go, and forgive me . . ."

The little courtesan had fallen back on the steps, and the blood that was flowing abundantly from her wound made her a crimson bed on which her beautiful pale amber body reposed in a regal glory.

"Oh, why does the happiness of some always cause the desolation of others?" said Ahmosis, placing her lips piously on those of her companion.

XIII

THE temple was surrounded, and all the doors were guarded by the satrap's soldiers.

Menonia, even prettier in death, reposed among the flowers. It was the festival of the goddess, and the courtesans had offered the young victim on the altar of amour in expiation of her sins.

Mylitta, the Lady of Sensual Pleasure and Justice, had to pardon the sacrilege committed in the sanctuary, and Zazai, the High Priestess, was exhorting her eloquently to clemency.

"Lady of all mercy and all bliss, do not condemn the courtesan who has faltered. She was the seduction of your reign, and thanks to her fervent ardor, many of the lords of Babylon laid superb offerings at your feet. The few jewels that she stole from you are very little by comparison with the riches her piety was worth to you. She has punished herself for her sin, and ought to repose in the earth of forgetfulness beneath the branches and the florescence that she loved."

At that moment, Himroud, her hair scattered and her veils ripped, hurtled into the temple.

"Flee!" she said. "The enemy has set fire to the external altars of Mylitta!"

"Flee? How?" said Zazai, calmly. "All the exits are guarded. Only the goddess can protect us; our existence is in her hands. May she watch over her daughters of amour."

She intoned the hymn of infinite bliss, and all the priestesses accompanied her with their passionate voices, as if death were alongside them.

The buildings that surrounded the sanctuary were already in flames; a red light passed over the faces in abrupt and fantastic jets. The fire played capriciously over the impassive idols standing in their golden sheaths.

"Flee!" repeated Himroud. "There are still the subterranean tunnels and the water-gate, which only we know."

A dull rumble arrived from outside, as if the river were beating the walls.

The frightened courtesans ran to a secret stairway behind the statue of Mylitta, which plunged into the ground. One by one, they disappeared into the black hole, while the soldiers of the satrap, outside, broke down the doors.

The din of destruction dominated all other sounds, and the cries of the besiegers arrived distinctly at the ears of the daughters of amour. A kind of collapse was heard, as if the elements of the earth had returned to a primordial state. The bronze doors had given way, and the black men entered tumultuously in order to pillage the temple and overturn its idols.

The priestesses who had not been able to go down into the subterranean tunnel resisted bravely, fighting desperately, repelling with their frail arms the bloody weapons that descended upon them, but the charming bodies piled up at the feet of Mylitta, inundating the altar with their blood.

A warrior of tall stature with yellow eyes and a thick beard sought among the victims lifting up the dead and the dying, dragging the cadavers by the hair, turning them over and throwing them away with rage. Finally, he perceived the hidden stairway and plunged into it with a cry of triumph.

At the bottom of the steps, women were weeping desperately before the water-gate, for that exit, like all the others, as guarded; all escape had become impossible.

Ahassuru, whose soldiers had followed him, scythed at hazard the hands extended toward him, and the carnage continued, more sinister, in the barely-illuminated cellar, where all resistance was vain.

The satrap recognized Himroud, who was writhing and moaning, imploring his pity.

"Where is Ahmosis?" he demanded, putting his foot on the young woman's breast.

"I don't know," she murmured. "A little while ago she was still in our midst. By the desire I inspired in you, don't do me any harm! Remember that I've been your wife, that you've held me in your arms!"

"Where is Ahmosis hiding?" demanded the satrap again, furiously. "I've searched for her in vain among the daughters of Mylitta."

Himroud, sobbing, raised her suppliant hands toward him. But with a rapid sweep, he slashed the two wrists, and floods of blood spurted from the supple arms, which fell back like broken stems.

"Mercy!" the young woman sobbed.

"All those who conspired against me have perished. I've had the accomplices of your flight crucified; I've had the prisoners and the slaves flayed alive. Only you and Ahmosis have escaped my resentment. It's necessary for my vengeance to be complete."

Hinroud lay at Ahassuru's feet, unconscious. He lifted her head and sliced through the neck, while his enraged men struck the kneeling priestesses, mad with terror.

Frantic cries, gasps and moans went up from all parts. In the midst of the flames, which licked the walls at times, there was a flight of frightful shadows, similar to non-existent beings of nightmare. The dementia of the murderers only calmed down when all the daughters of Mylitta, crushed, violated, torn apart and formless, lay in a red river that descended slowly from the altar toward the doors of the temple.

The fire, meanwhile, had respected the sanctuary, and, driven by a sinister wind, had reached the nearby houses. An entire quarter was soon ablaze, without it being possible to arrest the disaster.

Dream-like forms, incoherent and frantic, ran over the terraces. Every roar, every imprecation of the crowd, accused Mylitta of that new crime; a macabre fear ran from neighbor to neighbor, and Ahassuru, gorged on massacres, sated by murders and death-throes, listened to those voices, which were cursing and blaspheming in the firelight.

He was almost glad to feel himself cradled on the great river of light that was marching toward the king's palace, doubtless going to finish what madness had commenced. The cruel monarch, too, was insulting the gods in a last revolt of his obscured brain, feeling the stifling cloak of divine chastisement falling upon his shoulders.

Ahassuru, on the terrace of the temple, was enjoying his triumph ferociously when he suddenly uttered a scream of pain. Myrr, the great bird of prey, who had been flying grimly through the smoking ruins since the death of Himroud, had fallen upon his head, and, digging his talons into his skull, had punctured his eyes.

While the homicidal horror of a barbaric people was exalted, a delirious king was imprisoned in his palace and a cruel satrap was writhing in impotent rage, Ahmosis, lying in the bottom of Starzo's boat, quit the city of debauchery and crime.

Having been the first to reach the water-gate, she had been able to climb into the narrow skiff that was waiting for her, lost in the shadows, and, by means of the strength of his oars, her lover had drawn away from the accursed shore. The frail craft glided smoothly, furtive and silent, carrying away a human felicity.

She was going toward deliverance, toward forgetfulness, and the priestess of amour, her eyes closed and her soul sunlit, lay at the feet of the Beloved, hoping soon to see again the land of the Pharaohs, so mild and so magnificent. There, the colossi of stone, the crouching sphinxes with the mysterious smiles, would preserve them from the assaults of the wicked, for they were beings of justice, strength and clemency.

Ahmosis expected of their sovereign protection the assistance of which she had need; she felt capable of supporting the fatigues of the long voyage in order to attain the great repose of satisfied amour.

"I adore you," she said, raising herself up toward Starzo.

And in the formidable apotheosis of the city in flames, they exchanged a long and delicious kiss . . .

FREDERICK ROLFE (Baron Corvo) *An Ossuary of the North Lagoon and Other Stories*
JASON ROLFE *An Archive of Human Nonsense*
ARNAUD RYKNER *The Last Train*
MARCEL SCHWOB *The Assassins and Other Stories*
MARCEL SCHWOB *Double Heart*
CHRISTIAN HEINRICH SPIESS *The Dwarf of Westerbourg*
BRIAN STABLEFORD (editor) *Decadence and Symbolism: A Showcase Anthology*
BRIAN STABLEFORD (editor) *The Snuggly Satyricon*
BRIAN STABLEFORD (editor) *The Snuggly Satanicon*
BRIAN STABLEFORD *Spirits of the Vasty Deep*
COUNT ERIC STENBOCK *Love, Sleep & Dreams*
COUNT ERIC STENBOCK *Myrtle, Rue & Cypress*
COUNT ERIC STENBOCK *The Shadow of Death*
COUNT ERIC STENBOCK *Studies of Death*
MONTAGUE SUMMERS *The Bride of Christ and Other Fictions*
MONTAGUE SUMMERS *Six Ghost Stories*
GILBERT-AUGUSTIN THIERRY *The Blonde Tress and The Mask*
GILBERT-AUGUSTIN THIERRY *Reincarnation and Redemption*
DOUGLAS THOMPSON *The Fallen West*
TOADHOUSE *Gone Fishing with Samy Rosenstock*
TOADHOUSE *Living and Dying in a Mind Field*
TOADHOUSE *What Makes the Wave Break?*
LÉO TRÉZENIK *Decadent Prose Pieces*
RUGGERO VASARI *Raun*
ILARIE VORONCA *The Confession of a False Soul*
JANE DE LA VAUDÈRE *The Demi-Sexes and The Androgynes*
JANE DE LA VAUDÈRE *The Double Star and Other Occult Fantasies*
JANE DE LA VAUDÈRE *The Mystery of Kama and Brahma's Courtesans*
JANE DE LA VAUDÈRE *Three Flowers and The King of Siam's Amazon*
JANE DE LA VAUDÈRE *The Witch of Ecbatana and The Virgin of Israel*
AUGUSTE VILLIERS DE L'ISLE-ADAM *Isis*
RENÉE VIVIEN AND HÉLÈNE DE ZUYLEN DE NYEVELT *Faustina and Other Stories*
RENÉE VIVIEN *Lilith's Legacy*
RENÉE VIVIEN *A Woman Appeared to Me*
ILARIE VORONCA *The Confession of a False Soul*
ILARIE VORONCA *The Key to Reality*
TERESA WILMS MONTT *In the Stillness of Marble*
TERESA WILMS MONTT *Sentimental Doubts*
KAREL VAN DE WOESTIJNE *The Dying Peasant*